'You must be the Ice Fairy.'

As he spoke, one of the nurses standing behind Darla suddenly started to choke. The man held out his hand, seemingly not at all scared of her. Darla slid her hand into his outstretched one, ensuring the shake was firm and direct. She went to withdraw her hand, ignoring the momentary warmth his touch had evoked, but he stepped forward and warmly cupped her hand in both of his.

'A little icy—but then the air-conditioning can get rather cold in here. Especially if you've been sitting in your office poring over case-notes,' he stated, his gaze flicking to the pile of notes she'd left on the desk. 'And I thought fairies were supposed to be sweet and happy and loving.' He smiled at her, dazzling Darla with his straight white teeth—a perfect smile.

Her mouth went dry as she tried to control the unwanted sensations this stranger was evoking. As she wasn't all that experienced when it came to any sort of relationship, it took her a few moments to realise the man was actually trying to *flirt* with her—and from the way she appeared to be affected by his nearness, his subtle spicy scent and the warmth of his hands over hers, she realised he was succeeding…

Dear Reader

Canberra is the capital of Australia, and it's where we spent quite a few of our teenage years, running amok and generally having a good time before settling down to the seriousness of life. It's a lovely city with great sights, great food and great people.

Canberra is also the closest capital city to the fictitious town of Oodnaminaby, the setting for our two previous books in the *Goldmark Family* series: THE BOSS SHE CAN'T RESIST and TAMING THE LONE DOC'S HEART.

When creating this story, we both knew Benedict Goldmark needed a woman who would challenge him. Beautiful Darla Fairlie was the answer. We did feel a little sorry for Darla as we really put her through the wringer, creating a past for her we wouldn't wish on anyone, but in doing so we were able to shed some light on a serious issue. Thank goodness Benedict came into Darla's life to help her let go of the memories that haunt her, to shine light into her world and help her step from *existing* to *living her life*.

Act Now is a fictitious organisation, but there are many organisations out there every night, helping and encouraging people to change their lives. They are the *real* unsung heroes.

We hope you enjoy Darla and Benedict's journey.

Warmest regards

Lucy Clark

DIAMOND RING
FOR THE ICE QUEEN

BY
LUCY CLARK

First published in Great Britain 2012
by Mills & Boon, an imprint of Harlequin (UK) Limited.
Harlequin (UK) Limited, Eton House, 18-24 Paradise Road,
Richmond, Surrey TW9 1SR

© Anne Clark & Peter Clark 2012

ISBN: 978 0 263 22871 7

Lucy Clark is actually a husband-and-wife writing team. They enjoy taking holidays with their children, during which they discuss and develop new ideas for their books using the fantastic Australian scenery. They use their daily walks to talk over characterisation and fine details of the wonderful stories they produce, and are avid movie buffs. They live on the edge of a popular wine district in South Australia with their two children, and enjoy spending family time together at weekends.

Recent titles by the same author:

THE BOSS SHE CAN'T RESIST
WEDDING ON THE BABY WARD
SPECIAL CARE BABY MIRACLE
DOCTOR DIAMOND IN THE ROUGH
THE DOCTOR'S SOCIETY SWEETHEART
THE DOCTOR'S DOUBLE TROUBLE

To the staff of the Whangarei Hospital.
Thank you for making my mother smile
on her voyage of discovery.
Ps 19:1

CHAPTER ONE

DARLA FAIRLIE was met with a round of girlish laughter as she walked into the accident and emergency department of Canberra General Hospital. The laughter was blended with a rich, deep, modulated voice. Darla scowled as she adjusted the armful of case-notes she carried and headed to the nurses' station determined to set things to rights. This was a busy hospital department, not a nightclub where they could all stand around laughing and joking.

Trying not to grind her teeth in frustration, Darla dumped the case-notes on the desk, the noise they made resounding beautifully and causing a few of the staff to jump. They spun around to see what was going on and when they all saw her—*their boss*—the mirth slid from their faces as they quickly busied themselves with work. They tided the desk, picked up the phone to make calls or headed to examination cubicles to check on patients. Busy little workers, keeping their ice fairy happy.

Satisfaction flowed calmly through her as she watched A and E return to its proper rhythm. The ice fairy was in her castle and she wasn't the type of matriarch to tolerate insubordination. She knew her staff called her that and she welcomed it, the name keeping a nice professional distance between herself and the rest of the A and E crew. As far as she was concerned, it was the only way to run an efficient and productive department. If they were scared of her, so be it.

The only person who didn't seem to be doing anything, didn't seem to be scurrying away, pretending to be at all busy, was a tall, dark and—she reluctantly admitted—handsome man who continued to lean against the desk, arms crossed over his chest, watching her with open interest.

Darla fixed him with a firm glare but he still didn't move. The realisation that she couldn't reduce him to a shrivelled mess with one of her withering stares was a little disconcerting. She had no idea who he was but the stethoscope around his neck gave the clear indication he was a doctor of some sort.

She straightened her shoulders and folded her arms firmly across her chest. 'If you've quite finished flirting with my female staff, I'd thank you kindly to head back to your own department.' She delivered her speech with ice to her words, hoping it would do the trick of removing the man, whose deep blue eyes seemed to be watching her with a hint of mockery.

'You must be the ice fairy.' As he spoke, one of the nurses standing behind Darla suddenly started to choke. The man held out his hand, seemingly not at all scared of her. Darla tried to quell her annoyance at his lack of fear. Logic dictated that if he was this relaxed around her, he must be someone of consequence. Someone from hospital administration? Had he been sent to evaluate her?

She'd been acting director of the accident and emergency department for twelve months now and although she had officially applied for the job in the hope of making it permanent, the hospital board had yet to make a decision. She knew they were waiting for the return of Dr Benedict Goldmark, who had been on sabbatical for the past twelve months. If Dr Goldmark wanted his job back, then she'd be forced to find a new job, to make way. If he didn't, the hospital would be insane to pass up an A and E specialist of her calibre running their A and E department.

Now she was faced with a man who didn't seem to care he was disrupting her staff and the best way to get rid of him quickly so she could concentrate on her job was to be polite. Darla slid her hand into his outstretched one, ensuring the shake was firm and direct. She went to withdraw her hand, ignoring the momentary warmth his touch had evoked, when he stepped forward and warmly cupped her hand in both of his.

'A little icy but, then, the air-conditioning can get rather cold in here, especially if you've been sitting in your office, poring over case-notes,' he stated, his gaze flicking to the pile of notes she'd left on the desk. 'And I thought fairies were supposed to be sweet and happy and loving.' He smiled politely, dazzling Darla with his straight white teeth—a perfect smile.

Her mouth went dry as she tried to control the unwanted sensations this stranger was evoking. Usually when a man showed the slightest bit of interest in her, Darla's defence was to shut him down, stat. However, if this man was here to review her, she needed to play her cards very carefully. So she ignored his subtle spicy scent and the warmth of his hands over hers and lifted her chin a little higher, narrowing her gaze but fixing her smile in place.

'So why do you suppose, Dr Darla Fairlie, the staff here thinks you have a heart of ice and glare of steel?' he continued, and with a shock she realised he was teasing her. Teasing her! Darla started to see red. How dared he come into *her* department and tease her in front of *her* staff? She may only be *acting* director but it was *her* department until she was told otherwise. Darla tightened her grip on the man's hand and held his gaze, ensuring her tone was controlled.

'You appear to have me at a disadvantage, Dr...?'

His smile increased and a deep chuckle filled the air around them. 'Oh, if I told you, it would spoil all my fun and I *am* having such a good time.'

Darla could hear the muffled twittering from behind her and realised this discourse was being eagerly observed by the staff presently on duty. They coughed and cleared their throats, disguising the fact that they were enjoying seeing their present leader, their boss, their ice fairy, being brought down a peg or two. Well, she wouldn't have it.

With her temper rising to an all-time high for the first time in well over a decade, Darla jerked her hand from his hold, relieved the contact had ended. Her main focus now was to regain power over the situation and as such it was best to deal with this larrikin in private. 'Why don't we continue this in my office?' Without another word, she turned and stalked away, ignoring the smattering of quiet female giggles. No doubt *he* had pulled some sort of face behind her back, bringing forth everyone else's mirth.

Darla ignored the pain that pierced her chest. She'd been laughed at many times, too numerous to mention, and she loathed being taken for a fool. Growing up, she'd often struggled to fit in at school, eventually deciding it wasn't worth the effort to form friendships with such shallow people. She'd learned at too young an age that everyone always had an agenda. Everyone always wanted something. Keeping to herself had been her only form of protection and over the years she'd managed to perfect it. Now, when she felt incredibly uncomfortable, she was able to detach her emotions from the situation and look logically at the facts. Distance. Focus. Self-control. Those were her staples.

Without checking to see if *he* was following, she continued towards her office, her back straight, her eyes focused on where she was going, her thoughts sorting themselves into a neat order. She swiped her pass-card through the slot in order to open her office door. It was only then she glanced over her shoulder and saw that he *had* indeed followed her but was definitely taking his time, dawdling along, waving a hello to a few people who passed him. Deciding he was taking too long, she let her office door close, determined he could jolly well knock and wait for her to admit him, rather than her waiting for him.

Settling herself behind her desk, she straightened her blotter even though it was already in perfect alignment and shifted her in-tray back half a centimetre. She tapped her foot beneath her desk. Where was he? Had he thought her closed door meant she'd changed her mind about talking to him?

Darla tried not to let her impatience win. Distance. Focus. Self-control. She closed her eyes for a moment, drew in a deep, calming breath and centred her thoughts. Upon hearing the sound of his deep voice outside her door, her eyes snapped open and she decided it was her turn to keep him waiting, picking up the phone to ring CCU and check on a patient who had come into A and E last night with cardiac arrhythmias. She watched her door as her call was connected to the ward. She waited for his knock on the wooden panel separating them. It didn't come.

'This is Dr Fairlie.' She spoke into the receiver once the call was answered. 'I wanted to check on Mrs—'

The next instant, Darla's office door opened and in he walked. Pass-card in hand. Eyes alive with repressed mirth. Whistling softly. She couldn't help it. She gaped, losing her train of thought as he clipped the pass-card to the pocket of his chambray shirt.

He stopped whistling the instant he realised she was on the phone. 'Sorry,' he whispered, and closed the door behind him, before looking around the room and smiling at the generic paintings on the wall and the single potted plant in the corner. The décor hadn't changed.

'Hello? Dr Fairlie?'

The ward sister's voice snapped Darla out of her confused stupor. 'Er...Mrs Carey. How is she?'

'Progressing nicely. I can email you her most recent report, if you'd like?' Sister offered.

'Thank you.' With that, Darla disconnected the call and stood, both hands flat on her perfectly clean blotter. '*Who* are you? *Why* do you have a pass-card to my office and how *dare* you speak to me like that in front of my staff? I do not tolerate insubordination in my department.'

'*Your* department?' He shook his head and turned to face her. 'Is that right?'

Darla stood there for a split second, looking at him as though he'd grown an extra head. Slowly, she began to process his words and as she did, all the fire seemed to drain out of her as she realised *exactly* who he was. After all, who else would have a pass-card to this office but the man whose job she'd been babysitting for the past twelve months?

Straightening her shoulders and meeting his gaze, she spoke clearly. 'Dr Goldmark, I presume.'

He spread his arms wide and turned slowly in a circle. The open gesture gave Darla the opportunity to really look at him and when he was facing her again she wished he hadn't. Her gaze had quickly taken in the breadth of his shoulders, the length of his legs, the firmness of his torso and the humour in his eyes. 'In the flesh and…' he performed a little bow '…at your service.'

He was handsome and he knew it. The realisation was enough to help clear her thoughts from the vision before her. She slowly eased herself down into her chair—which she realised was really *his* chair—and clasped her hands calmly in front of her.

'You weren't expected until tomorrow,' she stated.

'Well…' He settled himself in one of the two chairs located on the other side of her desk. 'I was in hospital Admin, completing the mounds of paperwork so I was all ready to begin my shift tomorrow, when I decided just to stop by and say g'day to some of the staff.'

He'd been to the hospital administration department? Did that mean he'd made a decision? Was he going to resume his previous post as director or not? She hated feeling so conflicted in her thoughts and emotions but until she knew for sure, she needed to play it carefully.

'Saying g'day? From where I stood it looked more like you were disrupting the working environment.' She attempted to keep the censure from her tone but she wasn't sure she succeeded.

'Ah, that's because you didn't hear the great story I was telling. You see,' he continued when she didn't say anything more, 'when I was in Tarparnii, I was in the middle of nowhere, stitching up a man who'd been involved in an…altercation, when this monkey came along and—'

'I'm not particularly interested.' Darla's brisk tone cut through his words. 'Dr Goldmark, your—'

'Please, call me Benedict or Ben. Your choice. I answer to both. I also answer to "hey, you" and *"ea-wekapla"*, which is actually Tarparnese for "hey, you" and—'

'*Dr Goldmark!*' Her tone was filled with complete exasperation.

'Yes?' he answered innocently, realising he was starting to push her to the edge of sanity. He was intrigued by the woman who had taken over his job while he'd been on sabbatical and he was enjoying ruffling her feathers a bit, especially as it appeared most of the A and E staff were more than a little wary of her. In his opinion, that was the wrong way to be with staff. Being relaxed, having them on side, usually produced a more pleasant and productive working environment. However, when he'd been in Admin earlier that morning, he'd read the statistics for A and E during the past year and realised that under Darla's guidance things had been flowing smoothly. That news alone had helped solidify his decision not to resume the post of Director. Having been on a year-long sabbatical whilst working in Tarparnii with Pacific Medical Aid, where there had been very little red tape, had helped confirm that he could do without the excessive admin. He'd worked in Darla's job for almost two years before his life had changed but now was not the time to dwell on the past. Darla was talking and he'd do well to pay attention to the woman who was probably going to be his new boss.

'I am still acting director of this department until otherwise notified and as your shift doesn't officially start until tomorrow morning at seven o'clock, I would ask you to kindly leave the hospital immediately. I would also like to remind you that this is an accident and emergency department and as such staff are required to be one hundred per cent focused at all times.' Darla held his gaze firmly as she spoke. 'Something they don't seem able to do when you're around, joking and laughing with them.'

Benedict hung his head a little. 'You're right and I apologise. Consider me suitably chastised for my behaviour. Having worked in a loose and relaxed environment for the past year, I may have temporarily forgotten the protocols governing hospital departments. Rest assured, I will not forget them again.'

Darla breathed in a calming breath, pleased he was finally taking her seriously.

'However,' he continued, lifting his head, his blue eyes twinkling with delight, 'I'm sure you'll agree that during quiet times in A and E it's good for the staff to simply stop for five minutes, have a bit of a laugh together—which promotes unity and team bonding—ensuring they're not as fatigued, given laughter not only releases all those happy endorphins but loosens the body, and then return their focus to their work.'

'Ugh!' Darla stood and threw her hands in the air, shaking her head in total frustration. 'There's no getting through to you, is there?' she stated rhetorically. She planted her hands firmly on her hips and glared at him. 'This is still *my* department. You can't just waltz in here after twelve months of being away and think it's acceptable to upset the apple cart.'

'I wasn't trying to—'

'Quiet!'

There was a thread to the word that made Benedict

think he may have just pushed her a little too far. His older brother Edward had often said it was one of his worst traits, to needle and cajole until he went too far and often pushed the other person right over the edge. Of course, when he'd been growing up, usually the other person had been his younger brother, Hamilton, but Benedict actually couldn't remember needling anyone like this for years. He was a trained A and E professional who was good at his job. The way he was behaving with the stunning Darla Fairlie was even starting to puzzle him, but for some reason he didn't seem able to stop.

He'd spoken to a few of his Canberra General colleagues during the past year and whilst they all respected Darla in a professional capacity, none of them actually knew much about her. She ran her department like clockwork and kept her emotional distance from all staff. Why was that?

'But she's a good-looking woman,' Matt, one of his colleagues, had stated. 'A real beauty with her blonde hair and brown eyes.'

'You're a married man,' Benedict had pointed out.

'Very happily married, too, but that doesn't mean I can't appreciate a woman's beauty,' Matt had continued. 'She's a brilliant doctor, runs a tight department, is talented with administration and arbitrates disputes with an intense fairness. She keeps to herself, though. She's been here almost a year and none of us really know her.'

'So the staff respect her but don't like her?'

'Basically, yeah.'

It was why he'd decided to visit A and E after his meetings. He'd wanted to see the ice fairy in action, to get a fix on how she really behaved, and he had to admit, she'd given him a run for his money. What he hadn't been prepared for was her classic beauty. Her slim figure was clothed in a power-suit and he couldn't help but be pleased that she'd chosen a skirt over trousers as it revealed her smooth legs, the sensible court shoes still managing to highlight the natural curve of her calves and ankles.

Her blonde hair was pulled back into a tight bun, which on someone else would have made them look washed out and austere but not Darla. With her head held high, revealing her long, perfect neck, her lips pursed, her chocolate-brown eyes glittering with anger, the hair-style complemented her overall look and she definitely portrayed the vision of a woman in power who knew exactly who she was—but did she? Perhaps her efforts to appear cool, calm and collected helped give her the confidence to run such a stressful department as A and E.

'Dr Goldmark,' she began, her tone clipped, brisk and direct. Benedict brought his thoughts back to the present and focused on what she was saying rather than intently watching the way her pink lips, which were covered in the mildest sheen of gloss, formed the words.

'That is quite enough. You may have been on sabbatical for the past twelve months and you may be coming back here to resume your duties as director, but until I am officially notified otherwise, this is still *my* department. You have no licence to swan in here and run roughshod over the governing rules and regulations such an intense department demands, and I would thank you to curb whatever natural impulses you seem to possess in regard to being an annoying presence whilst you are within hospital grounds.'

Darla kept her tone firm and clear as she continued to look directly into his hypnotic blue eyes. She hadn't missed the brief appraisal he'd given her and she'd flatly ignored the way her body had momentarily warmed at such an action. 'Understood?'

'Yes. But—'

'No.' She held up both her hands, palms out as though to stop him. 'No buts, Dr Goldmark.'

'But I was only going to—'

'I don't want to hear it.'

Benedict stopped and watched her closely for a moment before slowly nodding. He rose to his feet, thoughtfully stroking his chin with thumb and forefinger. 'You've made some valid points, Dr Fairlie. I'm presuming there's a list of all new departmental protocols somewhere?'

Darla frowned, unsure of his easy acquiescence. Was this another trick of some sort? Could she trust him? Did he want to look them over so he knew exactly which ones to revoke when he resumed his directorship duties? A fleeting sense of panic filled her. Had she been too overbearing with the man who could end up being *her* boss? 'Er…yes. There are.'

'Great.' Benedict rubbed his hands together. 'Then I look forward to discussing them with you at dinner tonight.' With a nod, he turned and took a few steps towards her door.

'Dinner?'

He turned back to face her, a wide smile on his handsome face. 'Yes, a working dinner, Dr Fairlie.' He spread his hands wide. 'We've both got to eat. Let's say seven o'clock? Across the road? *Delicioso?*'

With that, he opened the door and walked out without giving her the opportunity to turn him down, to tell him she didn't believe in 'working dinners' and that he'd be eating dinner by himself tonight. That was that.

CHAPTER TWO

It wasn't three minutes since Benedict Goldmark had walked out of her office when a 'code blue' was called.

Darla rushed from her office, heading towards the emergency bays, when she caught up with Matrice, the triage sister.

'Two ambulances. More on the way.' Matrice gave Darla a full update as they readied trauma rooms one and two.

'Call in extra staff and notify the orthopaedic department.' Darla pulled a protective gown over her clothes as the ambulance sirens drew ever closer.

'Report?' a deep familiar voice asked from behind her, and she turned to see Benedict Goldmark heading to the sink to wash his hands. She glared at him, almost desperate to dismiss him, to inform him they didn't need his help, that they could all cope quite well without him, but she also knew it would take a good twenty minutes or longer for extra staff to arrive. The patients were what mattered most and because of that, Benedict was a valuable asset. Professionally, she needed him. Personally, she wished he'd leave. Her world was nice, neat and ordered, or at least it had been until she'd encountered *him*.

'MVA between a tourist bus and a school bus. Both

drivers are badly injured, the school bus driver was thrown from the vehicle. There are two parents and a group of children still trapped in the bus but reports at this stage indicate they're not critically hurt.'

'No doubt they're in shock.' Benedict nodded. 'They'll come later. What else?'

'Whiplash injuries, lacerations. Thankfully the tourist bus was equipped with seat belts but the school bus wasn't.'

Benedict shook his head. 'Disgusting in this day and age.' The ambulance sirens had stopped and Benedict finished pulling on a protective gown and a pair of gloves.

'There are three children, aged...' Darla stopped and quickly scanned the piece of paper triage sister had handed her '...ten, eleven and ten, who have suspected multiple fractures. They're still at the crash site. Arriving now are the two bus drivers. From reports, the tourist bus driver is nowhere near as bad as the man thrown from the school bus. Benedict...' She glanced at him. 'You and I will take that patient. That way, we'll be finished sooner and readily available for the next lot of casualties.' She'd also be able to assess his skills, to see if he really was as good as she'd heard.

When she'd first arrived as acting director, so many staff had mentioned Benedict's skill, his attention to detail, his ability to adapt to whatever situation was presented. Darla was eager to see that in action because if she was forced to relinquish her hold on this department, she wanted to make sure the A and E was in good hands.

She turned to speak to Matrice, who was on her way to meet the ambulances. 'I want you and Dr Carmonti in TR2 as lead,' she said.

'Yes, Doctor,' Matrice replied, and within another few minutes, Benedict's first patient at Canberra General Hospital was wheeled into trauma room one. He couldn't help but wonder whether Darla had wanted to work with him so she could suss his technique, to see if he was worthy of returning to the fold. When she permitted him to take the lead, he knew he'd guessed right.

'Cross-type and match.'

'Get an IV line in.'

'What's his name?'

'Pupils equal and reacting to light.'

'Carlos? Carlos? Can you hear me?'

'BP is dropping.'

'Get that plasma going, stat.'

'Patient has voided.'

'Carlos? I'm Ben. You're safe now. We're going to take care of you.'

'He's moving. Fighting.'

'Hold him.'

'Carlos? I'm Ben. I'm a doctor. You're in hospital. Just relax. We're looking after you.'

'I'm Darla. Stay nice and still, Carlos.' Her sweet feminine voice seemed to calm the patient and Benedict was grateful for that. 'We're getting you something for the pain.'

'That's it. Nice and steady.' Ben glanced around the room at the staff, pleased to see no one had been hurt during Carlos's struggle. As the nurse finished cutting off what remained of Carlos's clothes, Benedict continued to treat his patient. Finally, things started to settle down.

'He's as stable as we can get him. Suspected fractures to the right ulna and radius; fractured left tibia and fibula; possible pelvic fracture.'

Carlos had a non-rebreather oxygen mask over his mouth and nose, his blood pressure was still low but stable. Benedict wrote up the radiology request forms, having momentarily forgotten that as he was now back in a hospital, the red tape and regulations had to be followed.

'Well done, Dr Goldmark,' Darla said without the slightest hint of praise in her voice as Carlos was wheeled off to the radiology department. Benedict raised an eyebrow as he pulled off his gloves and gown.

'Thanks for the approval, Dr Fairlie,' he returned, and Darla was almost sure he was teasing her. She hadn't been teased in a nice, friendly way much throughout her life. Most of the teasing she'd endured had been filled with ridicule and spite. She nodded once, unsure how to respond.

'And now that I've earned your positive opinion of my professional skills, I hope you'll agree to grace me with your presence at dinner tonight.'

When she looked away, trying desperately not to roll her eyes, Benedict wanted even more to obtain a firm positive that she'd come. He wanted to tell her himself that he'd already officially resigned as director and was more than happy to take the post of deputy director. First, though, he had to get her to agree to the dinner date.

'Seriously, Darla, think about it. Going over those new protocols with me is probably the only way you can be assured I know what the new rules are.'

'You're not a five-year-old, Dr Goldmark, and I don't see why I need to hold your hand and explain the meaning of life.'

Benedict couldn't help but smile. The ice fairy was definitely cute when her eyes flashed with defiance. He took a small step towards her. Although there were other staff in the room, they were busy tidying and cleaning, getting TR1 ready for the next patient. Benedict spoke softly, ensuring they weren't overheard. 'I've already heard the meaning-of-life talk, Darla. Why don't you skip straight to the good stuff—the birds and the bees?'

Darla gave an audible sigh. 'Don't you *ever* stop?'

'Only when I get my way. I know you plan to leave me sitting in that restaurant all alone, imagining me a fool. That's not going to happen.'

'You're wrong. I can always imagine you a fool.'

Benedict's rich laughter rang out at her dry words and Darla was astonished to find a warm and fuzzy sensation flooding through her at the sound. She'd made him laugh! As far as she was aware, she'd never made anyone laugh before. It was a nice feeling but she quashed it as quickly as it had come.

'I can't tonight,' she finally said, and momentarily closed her eyes.

'Really? Darn. I'm busy for the next two nights and by then…my bad habits may not be so easily altered.' Benedict knew it was a long shot but he now felt an urgency to get her to agree to have dinner with him. There was no doubt Darla was not only an exceptional doctor but a good administrator yet none of the A and E staff had a clue who she was, other than their brisk, efficient boss.

Who *was* Darla Fairlie? Why did she appear to be wound so tight? What had caused her to be this way? In his past relationship with Carolina, he'd been lax in asking too many questions, content to accept people as they appeared. Not that he was looking for any sort of personal relationship with Darla Fairlie, or anyone else for that matter.

Settling back into his Australian life after spending a year working in Tarparnii was important but he'd been made to look a fool in the past and he'd vowed never to allow that to happen again. He'd be required to work closely with Darla and the urge to know more about her was definitely spurring him on.

Her eyes snapped open and she looked at him. 'Fine. Seven o'clock. Don't be late.' She pointed to Carlos's case-notes. 'And get them written up. Stat.'

'Yes, Dr Fairlie.' He gave her a mock salute, which accompanied his wide grin, as she stalked from the room. He clicked his pen and opened the notes. 'Success!'

Benedict couldn't help keeping an eye on the door, watching for Darla's arrival. Would she really come? Was she a woman who kept her word? He guessed time would tell but in the meantime he'd continue to be cautious.

The emergencies that afternoon had meant his day hadn't turned out as planned but that was the life of a doctor. Over the years he'd learned to juggle the busy times with the quiet times, eating and sleeping when he had the opportunity, but during the past twelve months in Tarparnii he'd also learned how to appreciate down time far more. In the jungle he and the rest of the Pacific Medical Aid team worked as hard as any of the staff at a busy hospital but the quiet hours were spent swimming in the waterhole or joining in with the locals and village life. He'd learned how to bake flatbreads by hand, how to string flowers into garlands and how to climb a coconut palm tree without shoes. Life there had seemed to make sense and now that he'd returned to Australia he wondered how long it might take for him to feel that same sense of calm satisfaction.

Surely having dinner with a beautiful woman was a start, and whilst he acknowledged that Darla's looks weren't the real reason why he'd pressured her to have dinner with him, he wasn't about to kid himself into thinking they also had nothing to do with his decision. She was stunning, with her slim build, her blonde hair and rich brown eyes that seemed to be hiding all sorts of secrets. It was the secrets that had propelled him forward, his gut instincts telling him there was far more to her than met the eye. As they were going to be working closely together from now on, he wanted to know what those secrets were. He had learned the hard way that caution was necessary and, by golly, he was going to get to the bottom of whatever Darla was trying so desperately to conceal. So instead of heading back to the house he shared with his two brothers, Bartholomew and Hamilton, he'd come to the restaurant early, determined to watch every move she made so he could analyse it.

With the restaurant being situated across the road from the hospital, it was heavily populated with staff either just finishing or just beginning their day. Bacon and eggs were served alongside pizza and pasta. George, the proprietor, was in his element, greeting people and laughing his robust laugh. Everyone at the hospital knew George and George knew everyone at the hospital. Even tonight, when Benedict had walked through the door, George had greeted him like a long-lost friend, pleased to see him back home once more.

Benedict turned his head to glance at a table of nurses who were laughing and having a good time, obviously letting off steam after a hectic shift, but when he focused on the front door again, he noticed the woman he'd been waiting for was already heading in his direction. He sat up a little straighter in his seat, watching as George made a beeline to intercept her. He'd told the proprietor of their 'working dinner' and as George spoke warmly to Darla, he indicated the table across the room where Benedict was waiting.

Darla didn't even bother to glance in his direction, instead giving George her undivided attention. He watched as Darla spoke brightly to George and when she smiled Benedict's jaw almost dropped and he was positive his heart skipped a beat. What a vision of loveliness. The smile touched her mouth, curving her lips up at the edges, her eyes alive with sincere pleasure. With George, it was clear, she wasn't the strict and demanding ice fairy everyone knew at the hospital and Benedict realised he was catching a rare glimpse of the *real* Darla. He had to admit...she was breathtaking.

She was still wearing the same suit, with her hair still pulled back into its sensible style. In her elegant hands she carried a manila folder, her handbag on her shoulder. With George she was easy, relaxed, friendly, and Benedict wondered how he might get Darla to look at him in such a non-threatening way. It would be the best way to see what really lay beneath the surface.

He continued to watch her progress through the busy restaurant, her movements smooth and controlled, her spine straight, her shoulders back. She walked with purpose yet also seemed to glide with perfect grace.

'Here you are, Ms Darla.' George indicated the table where Benedict was sitting. Benedict quickly rose to his feet and moved swiftly around the table to hold Darla's chair for her, beating George.

'Ready?' George asked quietly, giving Benedict a little wink.

'Yes, thanks,' Benedict replied as he sat back down. George excused himself and the instant he was gone

Darla put the manila folder on the table between them, determined to establish an air of professionalism.

'I took the liberty of printing out all the A and E departmental protocols for us to go through, just to completely refresh your memory.' She glanced pointedly at her watch. 'I only have one hour so if we could get started, I'd appreciate it.'

'Are you sure you wouldn't like a drink first? Some wine perhaps? Or a beer?'

'I don't drink alcohol.'

'Really?' It was something personal about her and he filed the information away.

Darla half expected him to question her, to find out *why* she chose not to drink, but he didn't. Instead he simply nodded, accepting her statement, and offered her another choice.

'Soft drink, then? Mineral water?' As he spoke, a young teenage waiter came over to their table, and while she'd been about to tell Benedict she didn't want a drink, that she'd rather get their work out of the way so she could leave, she found herself ordering a glass of iced water.

'Make that two,' Benedict added, smiling at the waiter and offering his hand. The two men shook hands warmly. 'How are things going, Eamon? I heard you were working here.'

'Yeah. Good,' the teenager replied. 'George has been very patient. Teaching me stuff, you know?'

Benedict nodded. 'Well done. Keep up the good work, mate.'

When the young man had left, Darla slowly opened the manila folder. 'You know the waiter?'

Benedict shrugged. 'Sure. It's the first time I've seen

him in over a year.' He nodded. 'Good to see him turning his life around.'

Darla was intrigued by his statement, knowing a lot
of doctors wouldn't give the waiting staff the time of
day, apart from expecting them to do their job in as un-
obtrusive a manner as possible.

'So protocols,' Benedict continued, pointing to the
stack of papers before them. 'What changes have you
made to the department in my absence?'

Darla picked up the first piece of paper and handed it
to him. 'Wait a moment. You said *the* department. Not
my department.'

'I don't own the department, Darla. I merely work
there.'

'But most heads refer to departments as...' She
paused. 'I refer to it as *my* department.'

Benedict smiled. 'I know, and so you should.'

'Wait. What?' Clearly puzzled, she shifted in her
chair and leaned forward a little. 'What do you mean?'

'Ben? Ben, is that you?' A woman's voice cut through
her words and Benedict's attention was quickly drawn
from her. Darla tried to quell her impatience at the in-
terruption. Was Benedict trying to tell her that he didn't
want his job back? That instead of being *acting* head of
department, the job could be hers? Permanently?

'Jordie!' Benedict quickly stood and held his arms
out wide.

'It *is* you!' With delight, his good friend Jordanne
Page embraced him warmly. Darla tried not to frown
at the way the other woman appeared to be hugging
Benedict close. 'When did you get back?'

'Two days ago. Just enough time to get over jet lag
before starting at work.' With his arm still around

Jordanne's waist, he turned her to face Darla. 'Jordie, do you know Dr Darla Fairlie? She's the A and E director.'

Darla squared her shoulders. There. He'd done it again. Referred to the department as though it *was* hers. Was it? Had he decided he'd had enough of administration work and was instead more content to simply be a part of the department team rather than running it?

'No. We haven't met.' Jordanne disengaged herself and held her hand out to Darla, who accepted it in a daze of confusion.

'Jordanne's an orthopaedic surgeon who, alongside her husband, worked with me in Tarparnii for the first few months I was there.'

'Those were good times,' Jordanne sighed longingly. 'Such a beautiful place.'

'Jordanne and Alex are both orthopaedic consultants at the hospital,' Benedict continued.

'You've probably seen our names on operation lists and met our registrars but life gets so busy sometimes there just isn't time to meet everyone.' Jordanne laughed and released Darla's hand, then pointed to her table. 'I'd better get back to it. Just going over some things with my registrars and new interns. It was great to see you again, Benedict. Give me a call and we'll fix a time to get our families together for a meal.'

'Sounds great.' Benedict sat back down as Jordanne left and picked up the protocol Darla had handed him earlier.

He had a family? As far as Darla was aware, Benedict was single and very much unattached. 'You certainly seem popular.'

Benedict shrugged. 'When you've been away for twelve months, there's bound to be people to catch up with.' He glanced at the first protocol. 'Still, no rush.

Let's take a look at these changes.' He started read-ing, giving the document his undivided attention. It was what Darla had wanted, for him to be serious, to study the changes she'd made to the department, to approve of them, but now all she wanted was for him to answer the questions that were hammering around in her mind, causing her apprehension and underlying excitement to increase.

'Uh… Benedict, you were saying something before Jordanne came over,' she prompted, unsure exactly how to broach the subject. 'You've…implied… That is to say, you've sort of alluded to the fact that you no longer want—'

'Here's your water,' Eamon announced, and placed the two glasses on the table. 'Phew! Didn't spill a drop.'

Benedict looked up from the page he was reading and smiled brightly at the waiter.

'Good lad,' Benedict praised, and then pointed. 'And here comes George.'

Darla glanced over her shoulder to see George head-ing in their direction carrying two hot plates piled high with steaming, delicious-looking food.

'Excellent.' He placed the page back on top of the pile in the folder and closed it, shifting the file to the side of the table out of the way. 'I'm famished.'

Darla looked from George to Benedict, completely confused and unable to make sense of what was hap-pening. She'd come here to discuss the protocols with Benedict. Then he'd thrown out such disarming remarks that she wasn't sure what he'd meant, and now George was bringing them food?

'Here you go, fairy princess,' George said sweetly. '*Fettuccine alla panna* for you and for Dr Ben we have *spirelli caprisio*.'

'But…I didn't order anything!'

'I figured you'd be hungry. That was one gruelling session in A and E and you've no doubt been catching up on admin work before that,' Benedict replied. 'So I took the liberty of ordering for you and, well, George knows what you like so I left the selection up to him.' He breathed in the aroma. 'And you didn't disappoint, George. Thank you.'

George bowed his head, then left them alone. Darla sat there, too stunned at the unfolding events to move. Benedict picked up his glass of iced water to toast. 'Here's to fine dining in a rush,' he announced, and then instead of clinking glasses with her he gave her a wink and a smile.

The teasing action caused a rush of warmth to flood through her body and for a second she wasn't sure if it was because she was actually enjoying his confusing company or whether she was boiling mad at him. The latter. Of course it had to be the latter.

He was probably winding her up, throwing out ambiguous comments about the department to simply play a joke on her. Well, little did Benedict Goldmark know it but she was an expert at recovering from teasing, ill-timed jokes. It had happened all through her school years as well as throughout her home life. Being put down, being brushed aside, being thought *persona non grata* was something she'd lived with for so long, she knew how to deal with it.

Straightening her shoulders, she desperately tried to ignore the delicious aroma emanating from the food. It was true she still had a full night of work ahead of her and would probably find no other time to eat but she could resist. She had questions. The man sitting opposite her had the answers. She wasn't exactly sure why he'd asked her to meet him here but she intended to turn the situation to her advantage.

'Benedict.'

'Yes?' He started to eat, his eyes momentarily closing in delight at that first mouthful. He chewed then swallowed. 'Mmm. I'd forgotten how good the food tastes here.'

'Benedict.' This time she couldn't control the impatience in her tone.

'Yes?' He held her gaze this time, raising his eyebrow in surprise. Darla's determination faltered for a moment before she continued.

'Do you plan to resume your position as head of A and E?'

'No.' He scooped up another forkful and held it near his lips. 'I did try to mention it earlier today but, well, things don't always work out as planned.' He glanced down at her food. 'Aren't you going to eat?' he asked before continuing with his meal.

'What do you mean, "No"?'

Benedict chewed his mouthful thoughtfully before swallowing and saying, 'I'll tell you if you'll agree not to waste the delicious food in front of you. I know you're hungry.'

'How could you know that? You know nothing about me, Dr Goldmark.'

'I worked in your job for almost two years, Darla. I know how hectic it can be. Please eat. If not for me, for George?' Benedict indicated to where George was standing on the other side of the room, watching her with a concerned frown. 'He worries about you.'

'He shouldn't. I can take care of myself.' It was her policy not to rely on anyone else, not to expect favours from other people and to make do with what she had. It was the only way she could ensure she didn't get hurt.

'No one's saying you can't. Besides, it's nice to have someone worrying about you.'

'Just as long as their motives are visible,' she murmured, before reluctantly picking up the fork and starting to eat. At the first mouthful her entire body seemed to sigh with relief, the food absolutely delicious, as always.

'Ahh… Good.' He smiled across the table at her. 'I thought for a moment you might pick that up and throw it at me.'

'And waste food?'

Her reply made him smile. 'My mother used to say that good food was made to be enjoyed and she was right.'

Darla noted the use of the past tense and it intrigued her. On one hand, she didn't really want to know anything personal about Benedict, preferring to keep their relationship strictly professional, but, on the other hand, perhaps getting to know him a little better would help her to control him within the work environment. Logic won out.

'Your mother—she passed away?'

'Yes. When I was thirteen.'

'That must have been difficult.'

'Losing a parent is never easy and I lost both in one horrific accident.' He put down his fork and reached for his water glass, taking his time. 'Thankfully, I have three older brothers. Edward was twenty-four when it happened so he gave up everything, all his own dreams, to take over the family medical practice and to raise me and my younger brother, Hamilton.'

'Your parents were doctors?'

'Yes. They were killed in an avalanche whilst out on a medical emergency call.' There was no smile on Benedict's face now and Darla could hear the love for his parents radiating throughout his words. He was lucky. At least he'd *felt* parental love.

She clenched her jaw and rejected the dull ache of envy she had long conditioned herself to ignore. 'So, the job?'

Benedict watched her, noticing a fleeting look of pain in her eyes before it was pushed aside. He'd been right. There was a lot more to Darla Fairlie than first met the eye and he was even more intrigued than before.

'I informed the CEO this morning that I have no wish to continue as director. That, whilst I enjoy the work, I'd rather not be snowed in under a mound of paperwork. They've offered me the job of deputy director and I've accepted. As you'd be aware, they need to formally advertise the director position and someone will no doubt contact you tomorrow to inform you of the required protocols to follow in this instance.'

'And you're not pulling my leg? Teasing me? Having a laugh?'

Benedict was surprised at her question. 'Why would I do that?'

Darla dismissed the thought and shook her head, relaxing a little. He didn't want the job. She'd already sent her updated résumé to the CEO. She could breathe a little easier, confident of getting the job, a job she really liked.

They sat in silence for a minute, both of them eating, Benedict glancing at her, trying to read her emotions, but she appeared very adept at concealing them. Darla swallowed her mouthful and looked intently across the table at him.

'Why did you really ask me to join you, Benedict?' she asked, her voice soft and a little uncertain, as though she could sense he had an ulterior motive. 'I'm fairly sure it wasn't to discuss the protocols.'

'No. You're right. I've already read the updated ones. You've done a good job.'

'Then why?'

'Why?' Benedict put down his fork. 'Because you intrigue me, Darla, and when I'm intrigued, I can't help but discover why.'

Discover? That was the last thing she wanted. To have someone as handsome and as enigmatic as Benedict Goldmark poking around in her neatly controlled life. The fact that he was intrigued by her was reason enough to stand up right now and walk out, reason enough to maintain a clear professional distance from him, reason enough to ignore the way he'd started to get under her skin. Already he'd managed to rile her, to tease her, to make her *feel*. She didn't like to feel. Feelings clouded issues. Feelings let you down. Feelings got you hurt.

CHAPTER THREE

'YOU'RE very quiet tonight,' Hamilton remarked almost a week after Benedict had returned to Canberra. The two of them were sitting in a small first-aid van, stocked with medical supplies, waiting for patients. Benedict looked over at his younger brother and frowned a little.

Hamilton shrugged in defence of his statement. 'What? This is the first real chance we've had to catch up since you returned and usually when you get back from Tarparnii you're always Mr Chatty, telling me all about your wacky escapades there.' Hamilton sighed with longing. 'I can't wait to go back. How was Nilly?'

'Nilly was great. In good health. Always shiny,' Benedict replied, smiling at the memory of their good friend who was matriarch of the village they usually used as their base for medical clinics when they were in the small Pacific Island of Tarparnii. Belonging, being grounded, surrounding himself with people he loved, was Benedict's idea of happiness. He had a great family and knew he was a fortunate man. He didn't ever want to forget it, especially considering what had happened with Carolina.

He closed his eyes as she swam into focus. Dark hair, dark eyes and buried deep down beneath…a dark heart. Of course he hadn't known about that in the beginning.

No. Carolina had taken great pains to hide her true motives. She was a misguided woman who had made a fool out of him.

He pushed the memory away and opened his eyes, forcing himself to focus his thoughts. He checked his watch. It was still early yet. Only eleven o'clock in the evening. It usually wasn't until after two in the morning when people started arriving at the van, looking for help. Benedict had planned on getting some sleep before his volunteer shift began but an emergency case had come in to A and E just as he'd been about to leave. As Matt had called in sick, Benedict had decided to stick around the hospital and help out. He'd also hoped Darla would finish up her meetings early so they could chat.

The woman was beautiful, intelligent and also highly intriguing. He could tell she was hiding something but he had no idea what. As far as work went, she was excellent both in administration and in dealing with the patients. He'd been very impressed and had also mentioned these facts to the CEO. It didn't matter that Benedict had been unable to stop himself from thinking about her during the quiet hours. The woman was intriguing. There were no two ways about it and the more he watched and listened to her, the more he wanted to uncover whatever it was she was trying to protect.

His colleague Matt had been right when he'd said Darla didn't mix with the other A and E staff. She was clear, concise and fair but Benedict hadn't seen her sitting in *Delicioso* with her registrars and interns, having an informal chat, as had his friend Jordanne. But, then, he shouldn't compare apples and oranges. Jordanne was a people person, so was his sister-in-law Honey, and, Benedict had to admit, so was he. He liked being around people, helping them both in a medical and mental capacity. It was why he'd taken the sabbatical, to go to Tarparnii and help people, especially when he hadn't felt too comfortable with the way his own life had turned out—thanks to Carolina.

'When you help other people,' he remembered his mother saying, 'you stop thinking about only yourself.' On that occasion, when she'd first said those words to him, Benedict had been about eight years old and his mother had been rushing about the house, checking her medical bag so she could go and deliver a baby. It had been his bedtime and he'd wanted her to stay and read him a story, to cuddle him and stroke his hair and kiss his forehead as she whispered lovingly, 'Goodnight, my Benny-boy.' As his father had also been out on an emergency call, it had fallen to one of his older brothers to make sure he and Hamilton got to bed on time.

As an adult, he understood what she'd meant and when he'd realised the truth of Carolina's duplicity, Benedict had taken his mother's advice and, instead of wallowing in his own misery, had taken a sabbatical to go and help others. It was why he was more than willing to continue volunteering with ACT NOW.

For years his older brother Bartholomew had been involved with ACT NOW, a Canberra-based agency that provided Nocturnal Outreach Welfare to those who needed it. Every night, there was a first-aid van and a van with hot food, coffee and even an array of clothing. There were vans situated in the north, the centre and the south of the Australian Capital Territory. The vans always rolled out together, usually carrying a total of six or seven volunteers each evening. Lawyers, medics, police officers, chaplains, as well as other volunteers with a heart to help were usually rostered on at least once a week, sometimes more.

Bart was presently at the food van, mixing and talking with some of the young adults who preferred hanging out with them until it was safe to head home.

'Once my old man's drunk himself stupid,' he could hear one boy saying, 'then I can sneak in and sleep in my bed, but if I go home too early, I'm nothing more than his punching bag.'

Benedict shook his head as the matter-of-fact words floated on the cool breeze. Hamilton, who was far more hot-headed than the rest of his brothers, growled with disgust.

'Those poor kids. Makes you realise how easy we had it, even after Mum and Dad died.'

Benedict nodded in agreement. 'You're helping, Ham,' Benedict pointed out. 'You're making a difference. Focus on that.'

'Yeah.'

The two of them sat in the van. Waiting. It had often been just the two of them doing things together when they'd been growing up. Out of the five Goldmark boys, they were the youngest and had often gone off on explorations together. After the deaths of their parents, they'd been raised by their older brothers, and family friends BJ and his daughter, Lorelai.

The five boys had stayed in their family home, continuing to live their lives, going to school and somehow managing to deal with their grief. His parents, Hannah and Cameron Goldmark, had been so happy together, filling their home with five rowdy boys and a lot of love and laughter. It was the ideal picture and one he realised he still wanted for himself, even after what had happened with Carolina. The question was, would he ever be able to really trust a woman again? For some strange reason, an image of Darla Fairlie entered his mind and he quickly sat up straighter in his chair.

He'd do well not to think about a woman he knew very little about. Wasn't that the way things had gone wrong with Carolina? Had he learned nothing from the pains of his past? Even though he'd been watching Darla throughout the week, watching the way she barely inter-acted with the staff but still managed to achieve good working results, keeping her departmental statistics up to their usual standard, Benedict had also noted she seemed to knowingly hold herself aloof.

He'd made the effort quite a few times to talk to her about non-hospital things, to ask her where she lived, whether she had any hobbies, any family, but to no avail. All he'd learned about her was that she didn't like to answer personal questions. She was closed off, cagey and cautious. She was hiding something and it was that which brought his distrust.

Most people liked talking about themselves, shar-ing anecdotes, telling jokes, laughing together. Those were natural human instincts yet Darla did none of those things and it was enough to keep him suspicious. It also made him more interested to discover exactly what she was trying to hide.

Carolina, on the other hand, had been bright, bubbly and bouncy, putting on a show to ensure she achieved her manipulated goals in the end—namely, securing herself a successful husband. As he'd been offered the position of director whilst still quite young, due to his experience working with ACT NOW and heading to Tarparnii as a medical student, Benedict's knowledge of emergency medicine had impressed the hospital board. Carolina had been impressed as well and he'd realised it hadn't been until he'd accepted the directorship that she'd really started paying him any serious attention.

Her deception had run deep and when all had finally been revealed, Benedict had come to see her for what she was—a conniving, manipulative liar who had confessed to never really loving him in the first place.

Why couldn't people simply be who they were? His parents had raised him to be true to himself, to be honest and to help others. Why couldn't he find a woman who was like that? One who didn't appear to have an agenda or an ulterior motive. He had always been so accepting, so willing to give people the benefit of the doubt, but that had been before his trust had been shattered. Now he had to tread carefully to avoid getting hurt. He didn't like it but he didn't see any way around it.

'Ham, do you think about Mum and Dad a lot any more?'

'Yes. Almost every day,' Hamilton replied. 'Although I was only nine when they died and my memories might not be as clear as those of the rest you, I had some great times with them both. Most of the time, though, I just wish they were here to talk to, not necessarily for guidance but just to talk, you know?'

'Yeah, mate. I know.'

Bart banged on the side of the first-aid van. 'You're up,' he called, and Benedict stood, having to bend his head down a little as he opened the door, which had been closed against the cool April evening.

'Hi,' Benedict said, smiling warmly at the woman who was being escorted by Yvonne, one of the other female volunteers. 'I'm Benedict. This is Hamilton. Come in. It's warm in here.' He held the door for the two women to come in. It was policy for a woman to always be present if the patient who came for help was female.

'This is Paloma,' Yvonne said and it wasn't until the two women were inside that Paloma opened the almost threadbare long winter coat she wore to reveal a six-month-old baby asleep in a papoose around her chest. 'And this is baby Frankie.'

'He's gorgeous,' Benedict said, then waited for Paloma to speak, to let them know why she'd come to the Nocturnal Outreach Welfare van. Benedict wasn't bothered by the silence. It was quite a common occurrence. People wanted help, were often desperate for it, but felt that if they gave in, if they revealed too much about themselves, that they'd be metaphorically pushed into a little box and shipped off to social services.

With two more people in the first-aid van, it was starting to become a little overcrowded so Hamilton quickly offered to get some soup. Paloma declined but Yvonne accepted, the experienced woman sharing a knowing look with Benedict and Hamilton. It was clear Paloma was cold, tired and hungry but felt highly self-conscious accepting the help NOW offered.

'Paloma's been sent by *the angel*,' Yvonne remarked seriously once Hamilton had left the van.

'The angel?' Benedict couldn't help the bewildered look on his face.

'She comes to the park, to the estates where she knows we live,' Paloma said quickly, as though she couldn't bear for Benedict to be ignorant of her. 'I don't know how she finds us but she does. She is an angel with her shiny hair and big brown eyes. She talks to us, tells us to get help, to get off the drugs, to think of our babies. She has fire in her voice like she knows what it's like, that sometimes there isn't a way out so you keep going on down and down.' Paloma stroked her sleeping son's downy head, her voice cracking as she spoke, emotion pouring from her words.

'She keep saying, "Think of the kids", "Think of the baby", "Think of Frankie". She say to me tonight, "Go to the van". I say to her, they will take my baby. They will take my Frankie.'

Paloma looked at him with pleading eyes. Benedict felt his sympathy for this brave woman increase.

'She says you don't do that. She says you can get me off the drugs and she says that you can keep my baby with me.' Paloma's eyes filled with tears and one ran down her cheek. 'Angels do not lie.' She kissed Frankie's head. 'I want to get clean. I want Frankie to be clean, too. I want to be a good mother.' Her eyes were pleading. 'Angels do not lie,' she repeated, her voice barely a whisper.

'No. They don't.' Benedict had no idea what all this angel talk meant but right now he didn't really care. Paloma had gathered her courage and come to them. She was trusting them and the next few minutes were crucial if they were going to be successful in helping her. 'Your…angel was right. At ACT NOW we have programmes that help mothers go through detox and stay clean, all the while keeping their children with them. We believe it's important the children be a part of the recovery so they can see that things are really going to change, that their mother is making the effort *for them*, for their future as well as her own. In Frankie's case, though, he'll need to go through detox too and for that he'll need to be closely monitored.'

'But you won't take him?' Her hands were wrapped firmly around the sleeping baby.

'No. He still needs you, Paloma. You're his mother.

He needs you to care for him. I presume you're still breast-feeding?'

Paloma nodded, the desperation in her eyes almost causing Benedict's heart to break. He smiled warmly and took her hand in his, giving it a reassuring squeeze. 'You're very brave. Coming here tonight would have been so difficult for you but you've done it. Your angel would be proud.'

He released her hand and reached in his pocket for his phone. 'First of all, let's get you sorted out with accommodation for tonight. There's a place specifically set aside for breast-feeding mothers but we won't be able to get you in there until tomorrow.' Benedict punched a number into his phone and smiled warmly at Paloma. 'We'll get you and Frankie sorted out,' he promised.

An hour later, Yvonne had taken Paloma and Frankie to the temporary night accommodation run by one of the local church groups as a women's shelter. Benedict had also been able to secure a permanent place for Paloma and Frankie over the next six months in one of the staffed houses where ACT NOW helped women in exactly this predicament.

He'd given both Paloma and Frankie a check-up and had just finished when Hamilton returned with warm soup and bread rolls for all of them. Benedict was pleased when Paloma accepted the food, eating as though she hadn't had anything for days. It was a sad predicament she was in but he wasn't here to judge, he was here to help.

'What I *don't* understand,' he said to Bart a while later, 'is the vision of the angel. Paloma was one hundred per cent certain she'd been visited by an angel and told to come here. Not that I'm quibbling,' he said, raising his hands to show he meant no disrespect. 'It's just…odd.'

'No, it's not. The "angel" isn't a vision, Ben, she's a real person,' Bart replied.

'Really? Does she work with ACT NOW?'

Bart shook his head. 'Nope. We've never met her, don't have a clue who she is but over the past twelve months we've had a dramatic increase in the number of single mothers coming to us for help. They all arrive here with the same story. A woman with blonde hair and brown eyes visits them. They say she seems to just *know* where they are, gives them an option to get out of their present despair, urging them to come to us for further assistance.' Bart sipped his warm cup of coffee. 'She somehow connects with these women, gets them to trust her and then sends them our way. It's as though she's that first step, that foot in the door. Not all the women who come here are addicts. Some are in abusive relationships and she offers them a safe way out. Others are homeless, often sheltering with their children in doorways because the temporary accommodation is overcrowded.'

Benedict listened intently to what his brother was saying. 'The past twelve months,' he muttered.

'Yep. Don't have a clue who she is or where she came from but with the results she's getting I don't care. As far as I'm concerned, she *is* an angel and she can continue on saving one woman after another, knowing she not only has our respect but our backing and support if ever she should need it.'

'I guess.' Benedict frowned, something niggling at the back of his mind, something obvious, but whatever it was it was slightly out of focus. He shook his head to clear his thoughts and looked over to where Hamilton was having twenty winks.

'Aw, poor little medical student,' he said softly, his tone laced with teasing. 'Wait until he's pulling all-night shifts in A and E. *Then* he'll know what exhaustion is.'

Bart chuckled but his laughter soon died at a loud commotion coming from outside, not too far away. Angry male voices, getting louder and louder. Hamilton sat up with a start and after a brief shared look, one that between brothers required no words, Benedict and Bart grabbed their coats and a medical kit and rushed out the door, leaving Hamilton to hold the fort.

The rest of the night ended up as busy as his afternoon at the hospital. The noise they'd heard had been a brawl between two rival gangs. Bart had called the police the instant they'd seen a number of men fighting. Benedict had called an ambulance as he was sure he'd seen the flash of metal, probably knives, as the violence had escalated.

After sending two gang members to A and E and several being taken away by the police, the dawn was well and truly upon them by the time Benedict was able to catch his breath.

'You did well for a man who's been used to lazing back in Tarparnii, sipping fresh coconut milk and applying the odd sticking plaster here and there to patients who've scraped their knees,' Bart joked, clapping Benedict on the back. He laughed at his brother's words, both of them knowing that providing medical aid in Tarparnii was nothing like that.

'Thanks.' Benedict yawned. 'I'm going to get some sleep. Ham, can I take your car?'

'Sure.' Hamilton tossed his brother the car keys. 'I'll

finish up with Bart. The car's parked two blocks down.'
Hamilton continued to give Benedict clear directions.
'And don't scratch the duco,' he continued. 'I still have
a few years to go before paying it off.'

Benedict laughed. 'A few more than a few, Ham.'

Hamilton shrugged but called after his brother, 'And
perhaps think about getting a car of your own, eh?'

Benedict nodded as he smothered another yawn, waving to his brothers as he headed off to find Hamilton's
car.

Two blocks down, he rounded the corner into the
street where Hamilton's shiny sports car waited and was
astonished to see a woman, slim build, wearing jeans,
boots and a long, thick jacket, on the other side of the
street, heading towards him. She'd pulled the hood of
her jacket over her head, obscuring her face. She took
keys from her pocket, pressed the button and the lights
of the car parked in front of Hamilton's flashed briefly.
Benedict watched her as she walked, checking the street
to make sure she wasn't being followed. The woman
appeared to be alone and he was instantly concerned
for her safety. She shouldn't be out here, on the streets,
alone, at this time. She could get hurt.

The woman's gaze was focused on the ground, con-
centrating as she walked. It wasn't until she went to
cross the road that she looked up to check for cars. It
was then she saw him. Her step faltered, just for a frac-
tion of a second, in the middle of the road before she actually stopped and stared at him. Did she think he was
some sort of lunatic? That she wouldn't be safe in his
presence?

'It's OK. I won't hurt you,' he said, and held up
Hamilton's car keys, jangling them in his hand before

pressing the button to unlock the sports car. 'I'm parked just here.'

'Of course I know you're not going to hurt me,' she retorted, and it was only then Benedict recognised her voice.

'Darla!'

She was the last person he'd expected to see walking the streets this early in the morning and, in fact, she'd been equally surprised to see him.

'What are you doing here, Dr Goldmark?'

'Er...' Benedict was too flummoxed to reply, still trying to process that the woman he'd thought about during the past week, more than he'd cared to admit, was now standing in front of him. 'Er...I could ask you the same question.'

'So ask.' It was only then she realised she was still standing in the middle of the road and, after checking for traffic, continued on towards her car.

'OK, then.' Benedict cleared his throat and took a few steps towards her. 'What are you doing here, in the middle of a deserted street at this ridiculous hour of the morning, Dr Fairlie?' And did it have something to do with the secret he could sense she was hiding?

She shrugged a shoulder, the action barely perceptible beneath her big jacket. 'Running some errands,' she remarked, and opened the driver's door.

'At five-thirty in the morning?' His tone was disbelieving.

'There are plenty of people who are up at this hour of the day.'

'Name three—and not emergency crews, that's too easy,' he said quickly.

'All right. Bakers, garbage men and radio show hosts. Satisfied?' Still standing, she slipped the key into the ignition then turned to face him, pulling the car door close around her body as though using it as a protective shield against the man who had annoyingly entered her thoughts far too many times since their impromptu dinner last week.

A small smile touched his lips. He couldn't help it. He liked her style. She wasn't going to let anyone intimidate her and he appreciated that. 'I guess I'll have to be.' The silence started to envelop them, the chirping of birds in the trees plus the sound of cars in the distance the only noises as they stood there, looking at each other. Where he'd felt utterly exhausted when he'd left his brothers only minutes ago, he now felt completely refreshed and restored. He couldn't deny that simply a few minutes in Darla's company had changed his mood. She was an enigma and one that seemed to be drawing him closer and pushing him away at the same time. It was an odd sensation.

'As we're both up and about, would you care to join me for breakfast?'

'How do you know I haven't had breakfast already?'

'Have you?'

Darla gritted her teeth, annoyed she couldn't lie to him and equally annoyed that he still didn't seem to read the 'keep away' sign she was desperately trying to project. She shook her head and the hood of her jacket fell backwards. 'You're obsessed with eating.'

Benedict looked at Darla, trying not to gasp at the lovely blonde locks flowing loosely about her face and shoulders. The early-morning sunlight glinted off her blonde hair and her tired brown eyes were looking at him as though she wished he would leave her alone. But he couldn't help but admire how incredibly stunning she was. 'It's something I tend to do a few times a day in order to fuel my body, but the fact that you're getting ready to drive away from me leads me to believe you're rejecting my generous offer of food, even after I've already proved myself to be a perfect dining companion.'

She tried not to smile at his words. What was it with this man that he wouldn't take no for an answer? He was her colleague and for all intents and purposes she was his boss. She didn't mix her professional and private life. In fact, she didn't mix her life at all. She had her work at the hospital and then her work here on the streets. Both were vitally important and the last thing she needed was to lose focus. The last time she'd lost her focus, she'd ended up with a broken heart and no job. She wasn't about to sacrifice her hard work just for a man. Never again.

'Maybe another time,' she mumbled as she tried to stifle a yawn. Darla climbed into the driver's seat, trying to ignore the fresh, earthy scent he wore, which seemed to be drugging her senses, wanting to know more about him, to discover why this man appeared intent on wanting to spend time with her. Although the morning was nice and crisp, there was a warmth emanating from him that was drawing her in.

Benedict stepped forward and grasped her car door before she could close it, stepping into the gap she'd just vacated. He crouched down so he was at her eye level.

'A rain-check? I'll hold you to that.'

'You do that.' She tried to convey nonchalance, his closeness starting to unsettle her.

'Seriously, Darla. It's not safe for a woman to be alone on the streets at this time of the morning.' His voice was soft, smooth and serious.

'I can look after myself.'

'Perhaps against one man. Maybe two, but tonight,

only a few blocks north-west of here, there was the be-
ginnings of a gang war. It wasn't pretty and it certainly
wasn't safe. Thankfully, the casualties weren't too bad
but a few were sent back to the hospital for surgery.'

Her eyes widened at this news, although she wasn't
startled by it. She'd seen many a gang war in her time
and she'd broken up plenty of fights. She also knew
when to walk away and hide. She'd become very good
at protecting herself.

'So you just happened to be passing by when this
gang war happened and stopped to lend a hand? Partying
hard with friends?' she queried, rubbing her hands together to indicate she was getting cold and he was blocking the means of her closing the car door.

Benedict frowned, unsure where her question had
come from. 'I was with my brothers.'

'Well, after your early-morning gang war patch-up
session, you're probably exhausted. I'll be expecting you
one hundred and ten per cent alert and ready for work at
one-thirty this afternoon, Dr Goldmark. No excuses.'

She was dismissing him—again. He found it quite en-
dearing. 'You're right.' As he straightened up, something
shiny hanging from her rear-vision mirror caught his
eye. A small crystal angel twirled in the early-morning
sunlight spreading out all around them. It was pretty.
Then he noticed a small angel badge pinned to the collar of her russet-red shirt, just visible beneath her jacket.

His eyes widened as his sluggish brain started to put
two and two together and come up with four. The angel.
Blonde hair. Brown eyes. Out at this ridiculous hour.
Cagey about what she'd been doing. Saying she could
look after herself.

'Oh, my gosh.' He stared at her for a moment, the
penny finally dropping.

'What? What is it?'

'It's you.' He stared at her in stunned disbelief. 'You're *the angel*!'

CHAPTER FOUR

'WHAT?' Darla simply stared at him in stunned disbelief. How could he have known? It wasn't a name she'd
given herself but after a few people had started calling her that, it had somehow seemed to catch on and
she hadn't been able to quash it. Truthfully, part of her
hadn't wanted to and when she'd seen the crystal angel
in the shop, she'd indulged herself and bought it, as well
as the lapel badge.

It felt nice to be needed, to know she really was doing
some good. She knew how these women felt, she knew
what they were going through, she knew what their children were going through, and it was her gift to be able
to help them in such a small way as to urge them to seek
help.

Her thoughts continued to tick over quickly as she
gaped at Benedict Goldmark. How had he clicked so
quickly and…? Wait a second. How did he know of *the
angel* in the first place? She pondered this for only a
moment before realising that if he knew of the mysterious and elusive *angel* then… 'You're working with ACT
NOW?'

'Yes.'

'You've done this…sort of work before?'

'Before I went to Tarparnii, yes, although my brothers, who also volunteer, have been telling me about the increase in women seeking help during the past twelve months. Those would be the same twelve months since you, dear Darla, arrived in Canberra. Even tonight a young woman, Paloma, came in with her tiny baby desperate for help.'

At this news he saw relief wash over Darla's face and if he'd had any doubts that she was indeed *the angel*, he didn't now. It also clarified that *this* was probably Darla's big secret. She would head out onto the streets at night, seeking out women who needed help, and she'd help them. Her secret was that she was working hard to make a difference in other people's lives, other people who were worse off than either of them.

Benedict's heart seemed to fill with pride on her behalf but still it didn't explain why she held herself so aloof at the hospital. Did she think people wouldn't understand her cause? Or perhaps they'd see her as some sort of modern-day saint? And why wasn't she working alongside ACT NOW as one of their volunteers? At any rate, Benedict was happy to note her motives were real, genuine and selfless. He'd seen first-hand what Darla's influence could produce and actions definitely spoke louder than words.

'Paloma and Frankie are safe,' he continued. 'One of our workers, Yvonne, has booked her into a temporary women's shelter for the night but later today she'll be taken to a small house and welcomed into a community of women who are not only in the same boat but also determined to fight for a better future for their families. And it's all thanks to you—angel Darla.'

He smiled at her, half puzzled, half impressed, and after a moment couldn't stop the question from tumbling off his tongue. 'Why don't you work with ACT NOW? Why do you do your angel work alone?'

'That's not what this is about.'

'Then what is it about?'

Darla rubbed her arms again, feeling more self-conscious rather than cold. There was no way she could tell Benedict why she did what she did, why she felt such a driving need to go around saving other women. There was no need to tell him it was her choice of penance for not being able to save her own mother.

She straightened her shoulders and lifted her chin with defiance. 'I really need to go. And so do you.' Darla met his gaze, trying to stare him down, to get him to move by sheer willpower.

He stayed where he was for a long moment before acquiescing. 'OK. You have a point. We both need sleep.' No sooner were the words out of his mouth than her stomach growled. She closed her eyes, unable to believe the betrayal of her own body. When she glanced up at Benedict, he'd raised his eyebrows. 'Are you sure I can't buy you breakfast? I know a nice little place, not far from here. Lovely food. Great big chocolate muffins. Hot coffee. Yum, yum.' He rubbed his stomach with his hand and she couldn't help the laughter that bubbled up.

'You are both persistent and quite silly, Dr Goldmark.' She shook her head in bemusement, unable to remember the last time a man had made her feel this way. It only served to reiterate what she'd been telling herself all week long—that Benedict Goldmark was a dangerous man to be around. He was nothing but another colleague. Period. 'I'm tired and I need sleep before starting work in a few hours' time.' She smothered a yawn. 'I don't have time to eat, please go away and leave me in peace.' Although she was chastising him, her tone didn't hold any hint of her earlier annoyance. All Benedict heard when she spoke was sheer exhaustion. 'I don't have the energy to argue with you.'

Benedict smiled. 'I'll remember that for future reference.' He held up his hand and ticked the points off. 'Doesn't drink alcohol. Guides women seeking help. Has a secret identity and when hungry doesn't have the energy to argue.' He smiled. 'See? I *am* getting to know you.'

Darla swallowed, a little scared to discover he was taking mental notes.

'Right you are, then, Dr Fairlie,' he said after a momentary pause. 'Away with you to your bed, and sleep.' With that he stepped back from the car and closed her door. 'And remember to drive safe,' he remarked, then whistled as he walked towards his brother's sports car, twirling the keys on his finger. He looked over his shoulder as Darla drove away, giving her a brief wave. He was sure if he'd pressed her just a little harder, she would have accepted his breakfast invitation. Still, the fact she hadn't, combined with the fact that he'd enjoyed having dinner with her, only made him look forward to the next time he could somehow get Darla to join him for a meal.

As he climbed into Hamilton's low-slung sports car, he pondered what the real reasons were for Darla not wanting to join ACT NOW. The organisation did a lot of good but they also had a lot of resources at their disposal. Darla was out and about on the streets by herself, in dangerous neighbourhoods all alone. It wasn't safe. Even ACT NOW operated under the policy that one person was never to go out into the streets by themselves. It was imperative they were either in pairs or in a group of three or more.

Even the ACT NOW vans travelled in pairs, the food and clothing van paired with a first-aid van. Safety in numbers. To think that Darla was out on these streets alone, by herself night after night, sent shivers of concern down his spine. He recalled Bart and Yvonne telling him of the good work the angel had done over the past twelve months, of the number of women and children she'd managed to help, and he couldn't figure out why Darla couldn't do all that good work with another person watching out for her.

He clenched his jaw and gripped the steering-wheel tighter as he drove through the quiet city streets, making a mental note to ask Darla those questions. For now, he'd do well to head home and get some sleep. His own stomach grumbled and he realised just how hungry he was. Perhaps he could stop at his favourite bakery on the way. Although the shop wouldn't be open yet, he was sure he could persuade his friend Tom to open up and give him something fresh from the ovens. His mouth watered as he thought about it.

'You don't know what you're missing, Darla,' he murmured to himself as he parked the car and made his way to the bakery, the scents of freshly cooked breads and cakes filling the air. The greengrocer next door was setting out his fresh fruit and vegetables for the day. It was while he was talking to Tom, sitting on a stool in the corner of the bakery, that Benedict was struck with a very good idea.

'If Dr Fairlie won't come out to breakfast...' He didn't finish the sentence but a wide grin spread across his face.

Darla wasn't sure how she managed to sleep after the night she'd had but for some reason the three hours she managed to squeeze in seemed to have rejuvenated her as never before. She hadn't planned on being out all night, it was just the way it had happened. Some nights she was able to talk to more women, to get through to them, and other times she felt as though she hadn't made any difference whatsoever. Those were the nights when she would come home early, the nights when she would sit and think things through, to figure out whether she needed to do something new or different. She'd think back to her own past, about what she'd been looking for back then, but that sort of digging usually left her with a terrible headache. It was her past that now drove her present life, which fuelled her burning desire to really help, but at the same time the last thing she wanted to think about was that horrific, upsetting and downright depressing time of her life.

Tonight, however, had been one of the good ones, and to hear Benedict saying that Paloma had followed through, that she'd sought out ACT NOW and had entered into their programmes, had been like music to Darla's ears. Even now, it made her smile to think she'd finally been able to get through to Paloma after months of talking to her. Paloma had done what was right and Benedict had been the doctor to accept her, to treat her and Frankie, ensuring they were placed into the correct housing situation.

Benedict. Why was it he had been her first thought when she'd woken this morning? As Darla walked towards the accident and emergency department, she rationalised he'd been the last person to annoy her before she'd gone to sleep so subconsciously it was natural he should be her first thought when she awoke. Yes. That had to be it.

Nothing at all to do with the way his smiles and his

rich, deep chuckles could cause butterflies to churn within the pit of her stomach. Or the way she'd been so incredibly close to accepting his offer of breakfast because if she had, she wouldn't be putting up with a growling stomach now. She'd only had time to sleep and shower before heading to the hospital, incredibly grateful her first meeting hadn't been scheduled until nine-thirty.

'Coffee,' she murmured, and stopped at the vending machine near her office, quickly inserting money and pressing buttons, but to no avail. She tried again but it didn't work, just ate her money. Her stomach growled and its impatience started to match her own mood.

Trying not to stomp like a five-year-old having a tantrum, she continued towards her office, her annoyance increasing when she discovered her secretary wasn't at the desk. What was the point in having one if she was never around?

Darla walked on and stopped short in the doorway of her office as she watched her secretary placing an enormous basket on the desk.

'What's all this?' Darla asked, and Syd turned around to face her.

'Dr Fairlie. You're just in time. This was just delivered for you and, my goodness, does it all smell perfect, or what?'

'Or what,' Darla replied drolly as she took a few more steps into her office. 'This' turned out to be a large wicker basket of delicious muffins—she could see at least four different varieties—with some fruit on the side, and, lo and behold... Was that a Thermos of coffee?

Darla could almost feel Syd looking at her, watching her every move. 'Uh...do you have the file for the departmental heads meeting? I'd like to review it before I leave.'

'Of course. I'll get it for you now.' Still beaming brightly, Syd headed for the door. 'There's a card,' she pointed out, a cheeky twinkle in her eyes, before closing the door behind her. Darla put down her bag and took off her coat and scarf before reaching for the card. There was no envelope to disguise who it was from and when she saw Benedict's bold, but surprisingly legible writing, she knew there'd be no keeping it from the rest of the A and E staff. By now Syd, a great disseminator of useless information, would have told anyone who would listen.

Darla clenched her jaw as she read what Benedict had written. 'I can still hear your stomach grumbling from here! Benedict.'

As though on cue, and probably due to the delicious scents emanating from the goodie basket, Darla's stomach grumbled. Why did he have to be so…considerate? She found it immensely annoying yet at the same time she was touched by his thoughtfulness. She'd been raised not to expect anything from anyone and she knew that on the few, very rare occasions she'd let her guard down, she'd ended up hurt.

And now here was Benedict Goldmark, being sweet and kind and thoughtful, and it was the last thing she wanted. He'd been back at the hospital for only a week and he was already creating havoc. Darla shook her head and walked slowly around to the other side of her desk, eyeing the basket carefully as though something bad might jump out at her any moment. Was this a practical joke of some kind? Were the muffins laced with laxatives?

Her stomach growled again and as she sat down in her

chair she pulled the basket closer, breathing in deeply. No. Although she wouldn't put schoolboy pranks past the likes of Benedict Goldmark, she honestly didn't think he'd be so cruel as to lace the muffins.

Where had he found them? How had he organised all this? She breathed in deeply again and this time felt her self-control snap. She was not only hungry, she was now starving. She had to keep reminding herself not to be drawn in by this smooth, handsome man she knew next to nothing about.

'Except for the way he wants to feed me all the time,' she murmured as she removed the Thermos from the basket. She unscrewed the lid and closed her eyes, almost sighing with relief as the scent of percolated coffee floated around her. Another minute later and she was sipping a cup of the piping-hot liquid and elegantly devouring a muffin. Then her phone rang. She quickly swallowed her mouthful before picking up the phone.

'Dr Fairlie.'

'Top of the morning to you—again.' Benedict's rich tones floated down the line. 'How did you sleep?'

'Fine.' She knew she shouldn't be curt with him but she couldn't help it. Every time he spoke to her or was near her or did something nice for her, she found herself completely off balance. For a woman who prided herself on always being in control, this wasn't a sensation she was enjoying. In her experience, men were only nice to you when they wanted something. So what *did* Benedict want?

'Did the basket arrive?'

'Yes.' A pause. Darla closed her eyes. 'Thank you, Benedict. You shouldn't have but…thank you.'

'Believe me, Darla, it was my pleasure. Anyway, I won't keep you. I'm presuming your schedule hasn't changed much from when I was doing the job and that would mean that Wednesday morning is the departmental heads meeting.'

'Correct.'

'Yep, I remember the drill, which is why I wanted to catch you before you left. I thought I'd check to see if things had gone according to plan.'

'And what plan is that?'

'The plan to make sure you eat more regularly. You see, Dr Fairlie, I think it's only right, as deputy director, to warn you I've appointed myself as your caretaker. I know how incredibly stressful your job is. I also know you don't seem to take a lot of time out for yourself, preferring to spend your evenings helping others. Anyway, after you drove away earlier this morning, after you flatly refused to indulge my whims and join me for breakfast…' His tone was become quite theatrical and Darla already felt her lips starting to twitch, just a little. 'And after breaking my heart and discarding me like…' He stopped. 'Oh, hold on,' he said in his normal voice. 'That was the one thing you *didn't* do.'

'Yet,' she added, and was rewarded with a deep chuckle for her efforts.

'Anyway,' he continued, his jovial tone coming down the line, making her feel all sweet and lovely and feminine, 'I was concerned you wouldn't get time to eat. That's all. Nothing sinister behind the gesture. Just wanted to make sure you had the opportunity to put some food in your belly so it didn't growl all the way through your meetings. Enjoy and I'll see you later.'

In another moment he'd disconnected the call, leaving Darla still completely perplexed as to what he was playing at. All men had agendas. All men manipulated women for their own selfish gains. Benedict Goldmark wasn't any different from any other male on the face of the earth…and she'd do well to remember that because right now, just for one split second, she desperately wanted to believe he was different.

'Benedict? Trauma Room Two,' the triage sister said when Benedict came back into the nurses' station, putting the case-notes he carried on the desk.

'Right you are, Matrice.' He pointed to the notes. 'I've finished writing those up. They can go to the ward with the patient.' With that he headed to TR2 to see what new emergency awaited his attention and was astonished to find Darla pulling on a pair of gloves and disposable gown. 'What are you still doing here?' he asked, his brow furrowing into a frown. 'It's almost six o'clock, Darla. You should have left at least half an hour ago.' He crossed to the sink to wash his hands and felt her cold stare digging into his back.

'You're not in charge any more, Dr Goldmark,' she remarked briskly. 'Kindly remember that.' She turned away and spoke to the attending nurses.

'Status?'

'Lydia Galgonthon. Twenty-one-year-old female. Ambulance called for by university. Patient was reportedly sitting and staring into space after her lecture ended, then collapsed. She briefly regained consciousness but was disoriented. According to paramedics, one of Lydia's fellow students mentioned she'd been involved in a car accident four months ago.'

'Do we have her hospital case-notes here yet?' Benedict asked as he came to stand beside Darla.

'They're on their way.'

'Obs.' Darla checked Lydia's pupils. 'Pupils equal and reacting to light.'

'Good.' Benedict looked at the treating nurse. 'Order an ECG, EEG and let's get an IV into her. Complete blood work-up to start with.'

As Heather, one of the nurses, started to wind the BP cuff around the patient's arm, Lydia started to shake and twitch, the muscle contractions increasing in severity with each passing second.

'She's fitting,' Darla stated. 'Benedict, check her airway.'

The nurses helped protect Lydia's arms and legs so she didn't hurt herself. Heather quickly loosened Lydia's clothing.

'Airway is currently clear,' he reported.

'Get ready to intubate if necessary.'

'Patient's voided,' Heather announced.

'Noted.'

'Two hundred mils of phenytoin, stat,' Benedict ordered. Once the injection was drawn up and administered, Lydia began to calm down, although her body was still alternating between rigidity and relaxation.

'Tonic-clonic seizure. First muscle contractions, followed by jerking,' Benedict remarked as Darla rechecked Lydia's airway and pupils.

'Airway is clear, pupils still equal and reacting to light. Lydia?' she called. 'Lydia, can you hear me?'

The patient started coughing.

'Take it easy,' Benedict soothed. 'You're in Canberra General Hospital, Lydia. You passed out at one of your lectures. Do you remember?'

Lydia opened her eyes, her gaze indicating complete confusion.

'It's all right, Lydia. I'm Benedict. This is Darla and together with our team of extraordinary nurses we're going to take care of you. You're all right now.' His tone was deep, placating and soothing. As he was speaking, Lydia tried to sit up but Darla eased her backwards.

'Rest now. Everything's fine. Just rest.' As Darla looked down at the young woman, Benedict watched his boss closely, at the way she seemed able to look right into the heart of their patient and out came such caring and genuine compassion. He had no idea how any of the staff could say her heart was only filled with ice. 'Dizzy?' Darla asked.

'Yes.' It was a whisper.

'Close your eyes for a moment. We're just waiting for your case-notes to come up from Medical Records. There are a few things we need to check.' They could ask Lydia their questions, such as whether she was allergic to anything or whether she'd sustained mild head trauma in her previous car accident, but as she was rather dazed at the moment, the information they received might not be accurate. No, it was better to wait for the notes. It was better to err on the side of caution, and as Lydia was now relatively stable, there was no need to rush.

'This is an oxygen mask, Lydia,' Benedict said as he gently placed the mask over Lydia's mouth and nose. 'Your oxygen level is a bit low.'

Darla put her fingers into Lydia's hands. 'Can you squeeze for me?' She did. 'Good.'

'Have you ever passed out before?' Benedict asked. 'No.'

'Have you ever had a seizure before?'

'No.' Lydia opened her eyes, her previously worried gaze now frantic. 'Not that I know of. How would I know?'

'Shh. It's all right. We're just checking.'

'Glasgow coma scale is thirteen,' Darla told Heather quietly, and the nurse noted the information. 'Lydia, is there someone we can call to let them know you're here?'

'My...my mum.'

'Your mum? Sure. Do you know her number?'

Lydia sighed, obviously exhausted from the seizure. 'My backpack.'

'In your backpack?' At Lydia's nod, Darla rested her hand on the woman's shoulder. 'We'll take care of it. You rest for now.'

Darla headed out to the nurses' station and Benedict followed, leaving Lydia in Heather's capable hands. Darla checked the local phone directory and found the number for the university. She picked up the phone but Benedict took it out of her hands.

'What are you doing? I need to get the contact details for Lydia's mother.' There was concern in her voice as well as annoyance.

'Breathe now, Dr Fairlie. Think. Surely one of Lydia's friends would have come with her to the hospital.' He angled his head to the side and listened. Darla frowned at him and snatched the receiver back, her impatience beginning to grow.

'Her mother needs to know.'

'Hark!' Benedict cupped his hand around his ear. 'What's that I hear out in the waiting room? Could it be the sound of concerned "Oh, my gosh"-ing by a gaggle of twenty-year-old females? I do believe it is.' He winked at her and headed towards the waiting room. Darla listened, then put the phone down, reluctantly following him.

He pushed open the door to the waiting room and there, in the corner, were four girls and one boy, backpacks surrounding them as they sat either talking or texting on their cellphones.

'Et voilà, chérie.' He smiled at Darla.

'I'm not your *chérie*,' she said between gritted teeth as she walked towards the students. 'Are you Lydia's friends?' she checked, one very small part of her wishing to prove Benedict wrong.

The texting and talking stopped as the collective turned to stare at her. 'Yes. Oh, my gosh, *yes*.'

'Is she all right?'

'What happened?'

'We were all so worried.'

'It was so freaky.'

Words tumbled out of their mouths and even when Darla tried to speak, none of them seemed to register what she was saying, they were all too caught up in their concern for their friend.

'Excuse me,' Benedict said calmly as he walked towards them. The deep resonance of his tone seemed to vibrate around them, causing their chatter to cease. 'Has anyone called Lydia's mother?'

'I have,' one girl said. 'She's on her way right now.'

'Should be here soon,' another volunteered.

'Can we see Lyds?'

'Not just yet but soon,' Darla answered. 'Did any of you bring Lydia's backpack to the hospital?'

'Yep, of course,' one girl said.

'Here it is,' another replied, handing the bag to Darla. 'Thanks.'

'Her phone's in the front section. Her mum's name is Irene.'

'Great. Thanks for that.' Darla turned and headed off.

'When can we see her?' one of the girls asked.

'We're all so worried. We need to see her or we won't sleep tonight.'

'I was so scared,' another repeated.

'I'm still shaking. Look at my hands. See? Does that mean I'm in shock?'

Their words filtered into background noise and Darla decided she'd leave Benedict to continue fielding their array of questions. After all, he'd proved himself to be such a dynamic people person, who was she to deny him the opportunity to use his natural talents?

CHAPTER FIVE

'NOT fair,' he murmured, coming to stand behind Darla as she read Lydia's EEG report. His voice was low and quiet but she could hear the hint of jesting in his tone. 'Leaving me to fend for myself. What sort of boss are you?'

'I'm the ice fairy, remember?' She turned her head to glance at him over her shoulder then immediately wished she hadn't. Not only could she feel the warmth emanating from his body, surrounding her with a delicious sense of protection such as she'd never felt before, but until she'd turned her head, she hadn't realised just how *close* he was.

Their gazes met and held, awareness surrounding them causing the atmosphere to thicken. It was similar to the moment she'd experienced earlier that morning when he'd knelt down beside her car, just before he'd realised she was the angel, although this one was far more intense. Benedict's blue eyes dipped momentarily to take in the plump contours of her mouth, before looking into her eyes once more. He swallowed, his Adam's apple sliding up and down his smooth neck, and she couldn't help but follow the action, her gaze resting on the undone top button of his shirt, his loose tie giving him a rakish look.

'What were you saying?' His whispered words were enough to snap Darla free from the intense atmosphere surrounding them. She looked down at the printout in her hands, the rest of TR2 coming back into focus. Heather was attending to Lydia, who was now dozing peacefully.

Darla cleared her throat. 'I'm sure, Dr Goldmark, you're more than capable of handling a small group of twenty-one-year-olds, especially when earlier this morning you were no doubt breaking up a gang war.' She tried to move away, to put some distance between them, but she didn't want him to think his nearness, the way the heat from his torso was emanating through her back, warming her all the way through, was causing her mind to falter.

'It wasn't a war, it was just a fight. Anyway, how does Lydia's EEG look?'

Darla thrust the readout into his hands and shifted to pick up the case-notes, glad of the excuse to put a bit of distance between them. She flatly ignored the way her heart rate had increased at being so near him, or the way his spicy scent still seemed to surround her, or the way she was having far more difficultly focusing her thoughts than usual.

'Nothing out of the ordinary,' she replied.

'Do we have blood results yet?' He reluctantly shifted his gaze from watching Darla, interested to note she seemed a little bit jumpy. Was it because she was tired? Or had she felt that burst of sensual awareness exploding around both of them when he'd whispered near her ear? Benedict forced himself to look to Heather, needing a reply to his question in order to click his mind back into professional mode.

'Not yet,' Heather replied.

'Do you want to do a CT or MRI?' he queried, turning to look at Darla again. She looked tired, exhausted, worn out and yet still managed to carry off her 'director' posture with finesse. At least he'd had the opportunity to get a good six hours' sleep before his shift had started. How long had Darla managed to rest? Since uncovering her secret, of finding out she was an honourable woman, it had been difficult to remove thoughts of her from his mind. Even when he'd been sleeping, he was positive he'd dreamt of her because when his alarm had woken him, Darla had been his first thought.

His previous caution, thinking she was another woman like Carolina who used others for their own gain, had been dismissed. According to his brother, ACT NOW had been actively receiving women who needed help, women who had been sent by the angel, for the past twelve months. Surely that proved she was not out for glory. For reasons still unbeknownst to him, Darla wanted to keep her activities under wraps, which only fuelled his curiosity further. She was an enigmatic woman and one he could now enjoy getting to know a little better. He knew she'd still keep him at a distance but the fact that he not only knew her secret but intended to honour it might surely bond them in some new way.

She was talking to him now, answering his question, and whilst he was looking at her lips, watching them move, he really wasn't paying attention, which was very unlike him. *Get a grip, Goldmark.* He focused in on what she was saying, knowing both she and their patient deserved his full attention.

'Depends on bloods and urinalysis. I've paged the neurology registrar, who's currently in Theatre, but he's asked us to organise Lydia's transfer to CCU.' Darla held out the case-notes to him. 'Here's the report from the road accident. Four months ago, Lydia sustained a head injury.'

Benedict raised his eyebrows in surprise. 'Could be the cause of the seizure.'

Darla nodded in agreement. 'We'll monitor her with that in mind. For now it's best if Lydia rests, giving her body time to recover.'

'And speaking of rest...' Benedict closed Lydia's notes and levelled Darla with a look '...it's time you went home, Dr Fairlie.'

'I don't think I need you—'

'How do you expect to boss and administrate and care for patients when you're burning the candle at both ends? I'm your deputy. I'm here to take over and do what needs to be done.' Benedict edged closer as he spoke. 'Everyone else in this department may be a little afraid of you but not me. Go home, Darla. Get some sleep, or I'll have Security escort you off the premises.'

Darla gaped at him. 'You wouldn't dare!'

He grinned. 'No, you're right, I wouldn't. Still...' He placed a hand on her shoulder '...be sensible, Darla. Have a good night's sleep.'

There was a caring tone to his words and for one brief second Darla allowed herself to believe it was real. To believe that here was an honest man who genuinely cared for her, rather than what he might be able to get from her. Was it true? Was Benedict a man of worth? A man of honour? A man she could come to trust?

Feeling her throat choke over with a surprising burst of emotion, Darla merely nodded and without another word walked from the room.

Two nights later, Benedict was once again rostered on with ACT NOW, working with Bartholomew and

Jordanne. Throughout the night, Benedict was rather quiet, both his brother and friend remarking on the fact.

'I'm allowed to be quiet now and then,' he defended himself when quizzed.

'Yeah, but why?' Bart asked.

Benedict tapped the side of his head. 'I've got a lot to think about.'

Jordanne looked at him closely for a moment before a wide smile broke over her face. 'Ah—it's a woman. You've met a woman and she's starting to tie you in knots.' She nodded. 'I remember that feeling. Oh, when Alex and I first met, the sparks were definitely flying.' Jordanne sighed and clasped her hands to her chest. 'For our first real date he took me to Mt Stromlo Observatory. What a magical night that was.' She shook her head. 'It was such a pity when the observatory burnt down in those terrible fires but at least we have our memories.' Jordanne blinked once, twice, clearing her thoughts from the past before fixing them squarely on Benedict. 'So…who's the lucky woman?'

'Are you really preoccupied with a woman, bro?' Bart grinned. 'Another Goldmark man bites the apple, eh?'

'Just because you've sworn to remain a bachelor,' Benedict countered, 'it doesn't mean the rest of us are following in your footsteps.'

'Aha!' Jordanne crowed. 'It *is* a woman that has you in a tizz.' She patted Benedict on the back. 'Well, good for you, mate.'

Bart continued to watch his brother, his smile turning into a concerned frown. 'What?' Benedict asked.

'It's not Carolina again, is it?'

'No,' Jordanne answered before Benedict could get a word in. 'It wouldn't be. That deceptive vixen took us all in. No, Ben isn't *that* stupid. Are you, Ben? It's not Carolina again, is it?'

Benedict laughed at Jordanne's complete turnaround. 'No, it's not Carolina. I've at last learnt to be cautious.'

'She was so sweet and kind and charming and all the while she was trying to work her way into marrying you, into conning you to open joint bank accounts together, to buy a house in both your names.'

Benedict shook his head, remembering. 'I was so close, too. So close to proposing to her, to signing the papers for the bank account, and we'd even started house-hunting.' He closed his eyes and shook his head. 'I was such a fool.'

'Hey—live and learn, buddy. So who's the lucky woman on your mind now? Must be someone special with the way you seem so preoccupied.'

'I'm *not* preoccupied.'

'You poured orange juice on your breakfast cereal, mate.' Bart laughed and Jordanne joined in.

'I'm just tired, that's all. Working at the hospital, volunteering here. I'm not used to it, especially after the more leisurely paced life I was living in Tarparnii,' Benedict offered, hoping desperately to throw both of them off the scent. 'In that glorious jungle, although the clinics are completely gruelling, there's generally quite a bit of time for rest and relaxation. Besides, the countryside is lush and green and—' He stopped as Jordanne sighed.

'Keep talking,' she said, resting her elbows on the table and propping her head up on her hands. 'I love that place. Alex and I are going back in another six months but just for a holiday this time. All of our children love it there.'

Benedict tidied up the van, almost wishing for an

emergency because he could feel his brother's sharp gaze boring into him. He'd been successful in distracting Jordanne but Bart knew him far too well.

'Yep, it's a woman,' Bart crowed. 'He's trying to change the subject.'

Benedict shook his head. 'I'm going to get some coffee,' he mumbled, needing to get some air before his brother pulled the truth from him. The truth was he was finding it nigh on impossible to stop thinking about Darla. He hadn't known her for that long but his mind was preoccupied with questions, wanting to discover more about her. Why was she so brisk and controlling in A and E, with her power suits and her hair all done up tight? Yet when she was out on the streets, she wore jeans and jumpers and hoodies and had her glorious hair flowing loose and free?

She was definitely good at her job, there was no doubt about that, but for some strange reason she seemed to prefer keeping her distance from the rest of the A and E staff. They all respected her but a few times he'd heard several members whining and muttering beneath their breath about her being too controlling. She helped people, both at the hospital and out here on the streets, yet she didn't seem at all interested in joining ACT NOW.

Was that because she liked to maintain control? At the hospital it was becoming increasingly difficult not to want to tease her. To see that glint in her eyes when he pushed her almost a step too far. When she nearly lost that tight grip on control and her brown eyes would flash with warning, her irises darkening as she glared at him. Her perfect lips would purse tightly as her exasperation blended with unwanted delight. Sometimes he had the impression she liked his teasing yet at other times he was sure if he kept on, she'd well and truly snap.

Outside the first-aid van, Benedict grabbed a coffee from the catering van then stood staring out at the darkened streets. The April morning cold didn't seem to affect him as he admitted to himself just how drawn he was to his new boss.

He closed his eyes for a moment, telling himself he needed to pull back, to remain professional and put some distance between himself and Darla. However, even thinking about leaving her alone caused his brow to furrow, especially when he knew she was out most nights, roaming these very streets. Her goals were admirable, wanting to help women, persuading them to seek a more permanent solution to their problems. He appreciated her drive to help those less fortunate than herself but it simply wasn't safe for her to go roaming the streets alone.

Benedict clenched his jaw and opened his eyes, struck with an overwhelming and powerful need to protect Darla. He knew she was out there, right now. He could almost feel her, just as he had the other day when he'd been standing close and she'd turned her head to look at him. If he'd leaned down, just a touch, their lips would have met. What would have happened next?

'She'd probably have walloped you across the face,' he muttered as he stood gazing out into the dark night.

There were all types of unstable people out at this time of early morning. She was probably somewhere, talking to a woman, urging her to seek help. Why was it she was filled with such a powerful desire to help? Usually if people wanted to help, they joined agencies such as ACT NOW, but not Darla. It was clear through her actions she preferred the one-on-one approach and only to women.

Why was that? Had something happened to her during her childhood? Bad experiences when she was young? Her determination was clear. He'd seen that on her face the instant he'd realised she was the angel, but what had sparked that determination?

For him, having his parents die when he was only thirteen years old had secured Benedict's need to be out here supporting ACT NOW in their good works. Lorelai and her father, BJ, as well as the rest of the township of Oodnaminaby, had been there to support the Goldmark boys as they'd all grieved. They'd offered help and advice with loving hearts. Even though it had been a time of complete tragedy and utter desolation, it had bonded them closer as a family and Benedict had long since told his older brothers, especially Edward, that he appreciated the sacrifices they'd made on his behalf.

He'd had loving people around him during the darkest moments of his life. Even when things had exploded with Carolina, Benedict had gone home to Ood and been welcomed by his family. He'd been blessed and he wanted to pass it on. If working with ACT NOW meant he could help even just one teenage boy find that same sense of security, to let them know they weren't alone, that they weren't useless and to help them see the world wasn't as unjust as they thought, then he'd be satisfied.

Benedict understood Darla's driving need and perhaps that was what had attracted him to her in the first place. She was beautiful, brisk and brilliant. He wondered if she was ever able to follow up on any of the women she'd helped. To see how well they were doing thanks to her encouragement. Did she ever see them

once they were involved in their life-changing programmes?

As one of the doctors working with ACT NOW,
Benedict had the opportunity to follow up with people
he met on these long and lonely nights. Over the years
he'd made lasting friendships with a lot of them, like
Eamon who had come to ACT NOW two years ago,
homeless and addicted to drugs and alcohol, but was
now clean, sober and working at *Delicioso*. There was
Keith, who at fifteen had come to ACT NOW after being
physically abused by his father and now, three years
later, was working with them to help other teenagers
who found themselves in a similar situation.

Even Paloma and little baby Frankie were doing well.
While detox was mentally, emotionally and physically
painful, Paloma was determined to see it through and
this morning, when he'd dropped around to the care
house to check on their progress, she'd told him that
when she was better, she wanted to help other women
like herself.

He'd been eager to share this news with Darla but
when he'd arrived at the hospital he'd been informed by
her secretary, Syd, that Darla was in meetings all day
and wouldn't be available until very late.

As Benedict sipped his coffee, he heard a noise coming from further up the dark street. His body tensed as
he listened, wondering if whoever was coming towards
them was friend or foe. When he heard the sound of a
young child's cry, he quickly finished his coffee and
tapped on the door of the medical van. 'We're up,' he
called.

'I'll get the soup ready,' Keith announced from the
catering van.

Jordanne came outside, shrugging into her coat.

'Where?' she asked, and looked in the direction Benedict indicated. 'Looks like a young mother with three children.'

'I see our mysterious angel has been hard at work again tonight,' Bart murmured. 'I wish we knew who she was so we could at least say thank you.'

'I don't think it's thanks she wants,' Benedict murmured as Jordanne went up the street to greet the woman, desperate to appear friendly without startling her. 'She just wants to see these women turn their lives around.' And he decided that for his next date with Darla he'd show her just how effective she'd been.

Of course, he couldn't tell her it was a date. She'd probably level him with one of her brisk stares before walking away, her back straight, her shoulders even. He smiled at the mental image in his mind.

'*The angel* sent me,' was all the woman said, her body language indicating she wasn't too sure she was doing the right thing.

Benedict smiled and nodded. 'That's what angels do. They show you the way.' And perhaps Darla was showing him the way to learn more about her. What was it that made an educated woman like Darla risk life and limb to go out night after night to help these women? Oh, yes, she was one intriguing woman and now that he'd decided on his next plan of action, he turned his full attention to helping the young woman Darla had sent their way.

It was another five days before Benedict was able to put his plan into action. He'd studied the rosters carefully and on Thursday afternoon noted both he and Darla finished their shifts at six o'clock in the evening. Perfect timing. He'd already spoken to the house manager where

Paloma and Frankie were doing exceptionally well to see if it was all right to bring a colleague around for a visit. He could just imagine Darla's happy face when she saw all those women she'd helped, to see the fruits of her labour, to know that she had been instrumental in changing their lives—for the better.

At the end of the day he found her in her office, locking files away and keeping everything neat and tidy.

'Wow. It's actually a *wooden* desk.' He nodded, completely impressed. 'When I had this office, I was never sure whether it was wood or plastic or made of glass because the paperwork was piled so high, I could never scratch the surface.'

'The paperwork isn't so bad, Benedict.' Darla couldn't help giving in to the small smile she would ordinarily try to hide from her colleagues. It was important she maintain her distance but with Benedict that distance didn't seem to happen. He had a way of invading her comfort zone, of barging his way in and refusing to take no for an answer. Part of her wanted to run away from him, as fast as she could, whilst the other part was impressed he wasn't intimidated by her, like other men.

He was more than capable of holding down a difficult job such as the one she was in and despite how he might jest of his time in the 'top job', when she'd taken over the position, she'd found the files up to date and neatly organised. He cared about those less fortunate than him, volunteering and getting his hands dirty rather than being the sort of man who did nothing more than donate money now and then. He was a good doctor, the way she'd seen him care about their patients, the way he put them at ease or gently extracted pertinent information.

In short, he was ideal and she'd idly wondered how

on earth he could still be single. She'd read his personnel file, just to double-check her information. Why she'd
done that was a constant topic of debate within her mind
but for now she was interested to discover why he was
loitering in her office when he should be going home.

'What do you want?' She picked up her large satchel
and started putting thick folders inside.

'Still haven't heard about the job yet?'

'No. I had my "official" interview yesterday.' She
shook her head. 'Can't they see I'm the right person for
this job? Why do I have to go through this rigmarole
every time?' The last phrase was muttered under her
breath but Benedict heard.

'Every time?'

She looked at him, ignoring his question. 'What do
you want, Benedict?'

He pointed to the files. 'A little light reading for tonight?'

'Yes. Don't change the subject. I need to leave almost
straight away.'

Benedict raised his eyebrows at this information. 'Do
you have a hot date?'

'No, but—'

He relaxed. 'Well, you do now.'

Her hands stilled and she glared at him. 'Pardon?'

'Come on. Get that bag packed. I need to take you
somewhere. Won't take long and I'll even promise to
feed you, but only if you're on your best behaviour.' He
came over to her desk and put the remaining file into
her satchel before picking it up.

'Benedict. No. I'm tired. I've had a hectic week
and—' Before she could utter another word, he'd placed
one finger over her lips, startling her into silence. He
leaned a little closer and looked into her eyes.

'I know you're tired and that you need sleep. I understand. This won't take long and it *is* important.' His gaze flicked to encompass her mouth where his finger lay. He quickly dropped his hand and shoved it into his pocket, the other gripping her satchel a little too firmly. What was it about this woman that seemed to draw him in? She had the ability to make all rational thought and the world around them disappear into oblivion, especially when he was this close to her.

It appeared she wasn't going to be able to wriggle her way out of whatever he had planned, which only proved just how exhausted she was. Ordinarily, she'd scowl at such high-handed behaviour but as she'd had a difficult time schooling her thoughts where Benedict was concerned, right now she felt it was easier to simply go with the flow. The sooner she appeased him, the sooner he'd take her home.

'All right.' She sighed as she picked up her keys and headed the long way around her desk, making every effort to avoid being close to him again. 'I'll follow you in my car.'

'Actually, I don't have a car yet. Keep meaning to buy one but haven't found the time. We'll need to take yours.'

'What about the—?'

'Sports car? That's my brother's.'

'Um…' She thought for a moment. 'Bartholomew, right? I've met him at the heads of departments meeting.'

'No. The car is Hamilton's. He's the youngest. Just finishing medical school.'

'How can he afford such a car?'

'By scrimping and saving. He's doing well.'

Glad of the neutral topic, Darla ensured her office

door was locked before walking out of the hospital, learning more about Benedict and his brothers.

'Proud of your brother?'

'Very. Ham is the youngest of the five. Edward is the oldest. Peter and Bart are twins. They're seven years older than me so between the three of them they simply took over when our parents died.'

Darla shook her head 'That must have been hard for you.'

'I thought so at the time, but now, seeing what some of these teenagers have to put up with from their parents and why they feel it's safer to live on the streets than at home, I can see I had it very easy. Surrounded by love.'

Darla sighed, her voice soft. 'That sounds nice.'

They climbed into her car, buckled up and as she pulled out of the doctors' car park she asked him to tell her more about his childhood. As she drove, Benedict shared some of his favourite anecdotes, amazing Darla at the way he could easily talk about his memories. He told her about the last camping trip he'd had with his father, going up to Mt Kosciuszko, the highest peak in Australia. He regaled her with some of the crazy stories from his recent trip to Tarparnii and it was then she learned he'd been to the Pacific island nation many times, first starting when he'd been a medical student.

'We have…extended family there, I guess you could call it. My brother-in-law, Woody, was initially married to a Tarparnian woman before she became sick and passed away. Then, Woody being Woody, he simply assumed responsibility for the rest of her family, ensuring he didn't bring dishonour to her mother and sisters. So I guess you can say there's a strong connection but we call each other "family".' He pointed to the road. 'Turn right at the next set of traffic lights.'

'Wait a second,' Darla said. 'I thought you said you only had brothers. How can you have a brother-in-law?'

'Woody? He's married to Lorelai. Lore is our surrogate sister. Her mother died when she was a young girl and my mother stepped into the breach. After my own mother's death Lorelai was really the only permanent female fixture in my life...well, until my brother Peter married Annabelle. Oh, and Woody's sister, Honey, is married to Edward.' He waved his hands in the air. 'It's all fiddly and complicated and...' he shrugged '...family-like.'

Darla slowed the car and put her indicator on, waiting to turn right. It was odd but hearing him speak made her wish for a family like his. All jumbled up and intertwined and happy, yet it seemed that she was always in the side lane, waiting to turn in the right direction but never managing to get to her destination.

'It sounds nice.' Her words were soft as the lights turned green and they continued on their way. Benedict looked at her as she cleared her throat and she couldn't believe how emotional she felt right now. It had been years since she'd sat down and allowed herself to wallow in misery at her unfortunate life but hearing Benedict talk so openly, displaying a clear love for his entire family, she couldn't help the strong surge of envy that passed through her.

'Slow down and take the next left. Third house down and we're there.'

Darla slowed the car and soon she'd brought it to a halt outside the house he'd indicated. 'So where are we and why?'

'It's almost time to tell you.' He opened the door and climbed out, coming around to her side to open the door for her, surprised when he startled her.

'What are you doing?'

He frowned. 'Opening your door for you. Helping you.'

'I don't need help,' she growled. And she didn't need him being nice to her either. Her life had been fine before Benedict had waltzed in and started turning it upside down, shaking things around and not seeming to care if bits and pieces came loose.

'You've forced me onto his wild-goose chase when all I want to do is go home and sleep for a few hours before head—'

'You're going back out tonight? Do you go every night?'

'I have to. What if tonight's the night some woman is ready to turn her life around? I can't allow that opportunity to pass by.' Darla stomped around to the footpath and indicated the house. 'So come on. What's this all about?'

Benedict's answer was to come and stand beside her, casually take her hand in his and then literally lead her up the garden path.

'Benedict?' she warned.

'Trust me,' he returned.

'No.' She shook her head for emphasis. 'I don't trust anyone.'

They stopped on the threshold and he looked down into her face. Tenderly, he raised one hand and cupped her cheek, his thumb gently brushing away the lone tear that was trying not to fall at one corner of her eyelashes. 'I'm really sorry to hear that,' he whispered.

CHAPTER SIX

EVEN though he hadn't knocked, the door opened and Benedict immediately dropped his hand back to his side, the tender moment with Darla broken.

'She is here. She is here. Oh, Dr Ben. Thank you so much for bring our *angel* to see us!' Paloma said, and before he knew what was happening, she'd reached out and pulled Darla to her in a warm, embracing hug. 'Thank you, angel. You saved my life.'

'Paloma!'

Benedict could hear the surprise in Darla's voice but it wasn't as bright and as cheerful and as happy as he'd thought it would be. He stayed back a step, watching as the other six women in the house came forward to greet her. The women hugged and thanked Darla for all she'd done for them, for helping them to see the light, for getting them on the straight and narrow, and the more they thanked her, the more Darla seemed to lock her smile in place and edge away from them.

'So that's the elusive angel,' Wanda, the house mother, stated.

'Uh…yeah.' It was then Benedict realised he might have blown Darla's cover. After all, if she'd wanted the workers with ACT NOW to know who she was, she would have told them months ago. 'But best keep that knowledge to yourself,' he muttered to Wanda. 'At least for now.'

Wanda held up her hands. 'If she wants to keep on playing super-hero, saving women and keeping her identity secret, that's fine by me. What's important are the women who need help.'

Benedict nodded, a little relieved to see Darla kneeling on the floor, interacting with one of the children. There was a smile on her face but it was a polite one, a stiff one, and again he was struck with the niggling sensation that he'd done the wrong thing in bringing her here.

'Oh, Dr Ben,' Paloma said, coming up to him and putting her arms around his waist. 'It is very wonderful. The angel, she says she is proud of me, that she is happy I am doing so well and that Frankie is looking more healthy.' Paloma pulled away and pointed to where Frankie was lying on the floor, gazing up at a toy frame, his little arms and legs kicking happily in the air. 'I promise the angel we will keep going, even though it is very hard sometimes. We *will* be clean, me and Frankie, and we *will* start the new life, the better life.'

At Paloma's words Benedict's doubts began to vanish. Even if Darla was a tad uncomfortable being here, he had to remember this wasn't about either of them. This visit was to strengthen these brave women, to show them there were people in this world willing to fight for them, to support them in their daily challenges and be proud of them when they accomplished more than they'd originally set out to do.

Thanks to Darla, little Frankie was not only going to get all those drugs out of his system and grow to be a healthy boy but he'd have a mother who was willing to work hard at providing a better future for him. Surely that gave her a sense of pride?

They stayed for fifteen minutes, both he and Darla talking to the women, playing with the children and encouraging them all to continue. The more he glanced at Darla, the more he sensed something was wrong, and when she announced it was time they were off because she had paperwork to complete, she gave a brief wave goodbye and was out the front door like a flash.

'Darla?' Benedict said a quick goodbye as well before hurrying out after her. 'Darla? What's wrong?'

'Why should anything be wrong?' she snapped, using that brisk, efficient tone he remembered from his first day at work. Darla tried to pull her car keys from her pocket but for some reason they kept getting stuck. In frustration, she stopped and placed both hands over her face. She hadn't wanted to lose control. She'd been trying so hard to remain calm, to not get angry, to be supportive of the women she'd helped, but the memories had swamped her the instant she'd set foot inside the house.

'Darla, what's wrong?' Benedict walked over and placed both hands on her shoulders, belatedly realising she was trembling. She instantly shrugged him away and took a few steps towards her car.

'Leave me alone,' she mumbled from beneath her hands.

'Pardon?'

Darla dropped her hands, anger, annoyance and anguish in her tone. 'I said, leave me alone.' Her tone was soft, almost too soft, as though she was so incredibly mad at him that all her temper-filled energy was being carefully suppressed. 'How dare you do something like this to me?'

'Something like what?' he asked, treading carefully and wishing to goodness he'd had more sisters instead of brothers. 'Bringing you to see a few women who were so desperate to thank you for everything you've done for them?' He spread his arms wide, still unsure what he'd done wrong.

'I don't want their thanks,' she told him.

'But surely you wanted to see how well they were doing? I saw that look on your face when I told you Paloma had come to see us at ACT NOW and that we'd been able to get her into a programme. I could see that you were happy to know the outcome.'

Darla glared at him as though he was incredibly stupid. 'It's not *seeing* the women that bothers me. Yes, I'm happy they've accepted help. Yes, I'm happy they're all doing exceptionally well, but that's not the point.'

Benedict spread his arms wide, completely perplexed. 'Then what *is* the point?'

She looked at him in disbelief, then shook her head. 'Forget it.' Darla turned and stalked to the car, walking around to the driver's side. Benedict followed.

'No. I won't forget it. I've obviously done something wrong and if you won't tell me what it is, how will I know not to do it again?'

Forcing herself to take calming breaths, Darla reached into her pocket and successfully pulled out her keys, eager to just get in her car and drive away, even though she was still trembling with repressed emotion. Going into that house, seeing those women there, the children… She leaned one hand on the car and closed her eyes against the images.

'Too many memories,' she whispered.

'What memories?'

Her eyes snapped open, not realising Benedict was

so close. She took a step back and pressed the button remote to unlock her car. 'It's nothing.'

'Darla.'

'Get out of my way, please?'

'Darla. Talk to me.'

'Why are you always blocking my way?' She reached out a hand to open the driver's door and again he noticed she was trembling.

'You're in no condition to drive,' he noted.

'Then you drive.' She surprised him further by tossing him the keys and stomping around to the passenger side, climbing in and shutting the door before he had time to compute what was happening.

Benedict opened the door and adjusted the seat. 'Sorry, but my long legs need a bit more room than yours.' He sat down and closed the door after him, both of them ensconced in the small, secluded cabin. Benedict didn't start the engine but instead turned to face her. 'Darla, I've obviously done something wrong, something to upset you, and I apologise—profusely—but how can I promise never to do it again if I don't know what it is I've done?'

'Why are you so interested in me?' The question sprang from her lips, as though her mind simply couldn't contain her curiosity any longer. 'Why?' she demanded again. 'From the moment we met, it's as though you've dogged my every move. Why? What is it you want from me?'

Benedict stared at her for a few seconds, his eyebrows raised at her questions. He could see she was trying to change the subject and he wasn't sure why. He wasn't sure of anything right now but he realised as he looked into her eyes that he owed her the whole truth, or at least the truth as far as he understood it. Darla wasn't like any woman he'd met before, which made her special… *very* special.

'I want your…time.' He shrugged, feeling exposed and a little self-conscious at this admission. 'I don't understand it myself, but from the moment we met I've had this burning need to spend time with you.'

'But *why*?' she implored.

'I don't know.' Benedict held his hands out. 'I like you. I think you're funny. You're intriguing. You're incredibly beautiful and talented and great with the patients and brilliant at your job.' The words seemed to tumble from his mouth, rushing over each other in eagerness to get out, to let Darla know that she wasn't like any other woman. 'You're unique.' He shrugged. 'I like unique.'

'You think I'm funny?'

Benedict smiled at her response. 'Out of all that, you only care about funny?'

'No one's ever told me I'm funny before.' She paused. 'You don't mean funny as in strange?'

'No.' He smiled brightly at her. 'You make me laugh, Darla. Your humour isn't silly, it's intelligent.' Feeling bold, he reached out and took one of her hands in his, pleased to see the trembling wasn't as bad as before. Whatever had riled her up was still present, he could feel it, but he was also beginning to discover there was even more to Darla Fairlie than met the eye and if he was going to uncover what that might be, he first needed to earn her trust.

'You run the A and E department with grace and elegance and you do a much better job of it than I ever did. You deserve that job.' She opened her mouth to protest and he quickly continued. 'And I'm not just saying that to be polite. I really mean it, Darla.'

She shook her head, as though she was finding it increasingly difficult to accept what he was saying. Benedict watched her response closely. She seemed annoyed when he tried to do something nice and embarrassed when he gave her compliments. Why?

'Darla, how many people have ever given you compliments before?'

'I don't believe in compliments.'

'That's not what I asked. I can see it makes you feel uncomfortable when I say nice things to you. Nice things you *deserve*.' The instant the words were out of his mouth, it was as though someone had switched on a light-bulb. 'Ah…that's why you were upset just now. That's why you were withdrawn when seeing the women. Their gratitude makes you feel uncomfortable.'

Benedict nodded as though things were finally starting to make a bit more sense. 'You help them because you feel you must but you don't want any thanks for it.' He nodded again. 'I guess that's also why you're an excellent A and E director. Patients come in, we patch them up and move them either to surgery, the ward, or they go home. No long-term care.'

Benedict was looking at her as though he'd managed to put another piece of the puzzle into place—the puzzle that was *her* life. Why was he so interested in her? Why couldn't he simply be like other colleagues who came to work, did what she told them to do and left her alone? She'd worked incredibly hard to erect firm barriers around her life so how could Benedict Goldmark waltz right in and start knocking them down?

'Why is it that you prefer to remain on the periphery?' he asked, and she felt like holding up her hands to hold him back, to keep him away from breaking down another wall. Her heart was starting to beat a little faster and she wasn't quite sure whether it was due to his nearness or the fact that he might just uncover the truth about her, because once he *did* uncover the truth, he wouldn't want anything to do with her. Wasn't that what she wanted? For Benedict to leave her alone? She tried to look away, to look down at their hands, past his shoulder, out the window into the early night surrounding them…but she couldn't. Blue eyes continued to bore into her soul as he verbalised his thoughts.

'Why is it that you work twice as hard as anyone else I've ever met? You're not burning the candle at both ends, you're burning a fuse, and you don't seem to care if it destroys you. Why?' He paused and peered closely at her for a moment, desperate to see further into her life. Then he pulled back, straightening up a little, but didn't release her hands. 'And why is it you now look like a startled rabbit? As though I'm trying to hunt you down and capture you?'

'Aren't you?'

'No.' Benedict raised her hand to his lips and brushed a soft kiss to her skin. 'I don't want to capture you, Darla. I simply want to know you better. I don't care about your past or the burdens you're carrying. We all have burdens but it does appear to me that whatever you felt in that house just now is related to your past. I don't know. It's just a hunch.' He cupped her hand with his other one. 'If you want to talk, just want to get it out, to unload, then I'm here for you. I'll listen.'

Darla pursed her lips together, feeling tears prick behind her eyes at his gentleness. She worked hard to control her breathing, to return her heart rate back to normal. 'What if I don't want to talk? What if I want to continue carrying my burdens on my own?' She tried to straighten her shoulders but it was difficult to do when he was holding her hand in his. Difficult to concentrate on anything when his thumb was gently caressing her skin. Difficult to forget the pact she'd made with herself all those long years ago never to trust or rely on anyone but herself.

'Then I'll loan you a forklift so you don't have to carry all that weight by yourself.' He was rewarded with a very small twitch of her lips into a smile. 'Seriously, though, Darla, your past is only one part of who you are. I'm interested in *you*. I want to get to know *you*.'

Darla listened to what he was saying, looked at the way he was gently caressing her hand. He'd asked for her time and he wanted to know more about her. She knew she was walking a tightrope but for the moment she at least had a safety net beneath. Things would never get serious with a man like Benedict Goldmark. She wouldn't let them. She would remain in control. So why couldn't she at least enjoy a small level of friendly companionship?

'Thirty-five A, West Fullarton Way,' she stated.

'Pardon?' Benedict looked at her as though she'd just spoke jibberish.

'It's my address.'

'Oh.' The grip on her hand, slackened a bit, as though he'd been expecting a completely different answer. Then it clicked. Darla wanted him to take her home. She was allowing him to do that for her. 'Oh!' His smile widened and he gently released her hand before turning to adjust the seat a tad more and then start the engine. 'Right. Home.'

'And I'm hungry,' she stated as they both pulled on their seat belts. 'You can buy me pizza.'

His smile was wide. 'Can I now?'

'Yes.' Darla's own smile became more pronounced as

Benedict pulled the car away from the kerb, away from the house that had seemed to swamp her with oppression. It wasn't Benedict's fault and it certainly wasn't the fault of the women who were staying there. Her stomach had growled and she'd realised she was hungry and tired. Having Benedict driving her home and enjoying a pizza with him were nice, calm activities that would help ease the tension she could feel tugging across her shoulders.

If Benedict held true to his statements that he wasn't interested in her past, that he wasn't going to try and pry into her life, then perhaps it was all right to give him the one thing he'd asked for—some of her time. Besides, at the moment she felt like a bit of light-hearted company and Benedict was just the man to provide it.

Within the hour, they were sitting on the floor of Darla's duplex, eating pizza.

'Why do you have so little furniture?' Benedict asked as he shifted around again, trying to get comfortable.

'I don't need much and nine times out of ten I'm usually only here to sleep.' It was on the tip of her tongue to tell him she had more furniture now than she'd had growing up. 'Besides, I'm still only *acting* director of A and E. If they appoint someone else to the role, I'll have to up and move. Again.'

'You've moved around a lot?' Benedict tried to sound calm, nonchalant, not wanting to scare her. Darla had relaxed somewhat since they'd arrived here and he didn't want her to startle her into silence.

'Uh…a bit. Melbourne. Sydney. Here.'

'That's not too bad. I lived all my life in one big country house until I came to Canberra to go to medical school and even then I still lived with my brothers.'

'You don't want to get a place of your own?'

'I had started looking…a while ago…before I went to Tarparnii.'

'And why did you go to Tarparnii for such a long time? You were director of A and E, a coveted position for a man so young, and then you up and leave? Something must have happened.'

Benedict shifted his position, sitting crossed-legged opposite her. 'Have you been checking up on me, Dr Fairlie? Reading my file?'

Darla felt a little uncomfortable that he'd rumbled her so quickly but she squared her shoulders, determined not to feel guilty. 'Of course I read your file. You're the new deputy director.'

Benedict stared at her for a moment before a slow smile spread across his face. 'Good answer.'

'So? Why did you leave?'

'The age-old answer, I'm afraid—a woman.'

'A woman? Really?'

'She tricked me, burned me and spurned me. Ripped my heart out and ate it—just for pleasure.' Benedict exhaled slowly, his smile completely gone. 'I needed to get away.'

'You ran away?'

'Yep, and I'm not ashamed to admit it. I needed space. I needed to be with people who loved me, people I could trust.' He nodded. 'Tarparnii was the best place to go because I could think things through supported by wise and wonderful people, as well as continuing to help out and provide medical care for those who need it.'

'It sounds lovely.'

'It is. You should go. Do a stint with PMA. You'll love it there.'

Darla shrugged a shoulder. 'I have work here. Important work. Helping women on the streets. Helping them to realise there's a better life for them, that they don't need to put up with living a second-rate life, that there is a life without abuse.'

Her words were vehement, strong, determined, and Benedict's previous hunch that she'd somehow been affected by this dark and desolate world increased. 'Understood,' he commented softly. 'But your work shouldn't define you. Being a doctor is just a job, Darla. An important one, no doubt, but no more important than the garbage collectors cleaning up our streets or the teachers educating young children or the mother who just wants the best for her child.'

He knew it was the wrong thing to say the instant her lips pursed together, making a tight line. 'I know you don't want to hear this. I know you're probably so used to everyone cowering at the sight of the great ice fairy and doing what you tell them but that doesn't work with me. I'm not trying to tell you what to do—'

'Oh, really?' she muttered, but knew he'd heard.

'Or what to think or how to live your life—'

'You could have fooled me.'

'But instead to help you see there is more to your life than just being a doctor, than just being the angel.'

'No, there isn't.'

'You work and you work, Darla,' he implored. 'But where do you live?'

She spread her arms wide to indicate the house. Benedict smiled sadly. 'This is just bricks and mortar.' He placed one hand over his heart, his eyes sad, his words imploring. 'Where is your heart, Darla? Why have you boxed it up and hidden it away?'

'That's… It has nothing to…do…'

'Who hurt you?'

'Too many people. All right?' She stood and crossed her arms firmly over her chest before stalking to the window, looking out at the dark and lonely night. It was how she felt. Dark and lonely. It was how she'd felt for years. Dark and lonely. It was how she'd always thought she would feel, so much so that she'd actually started getting used to it…hadn't she?

Now here was Benedict, asking her probing questions, digging into her life, into her past, even though he'd said he wasn't interested. Anger and pain, stronger than she'd thought possible, ripped through her. He'd lied to her. She shouldn't be surprised. Everyone lied. Always. Why had she somehow expected Benedict to be different? Why had she even contemplated being able to trust him?

'And this is you? Not prying into my past?' She didn't turn and face him, trying desperately to get her emotions under control.

'I said I didn't care about your past. A past is a past. You can't go back and change it but neither can you live there, and I'll admit,' he said, rising to his feet but making no effort to move closer, 'I'm curious about you, naturally, but the only reason I'd want to know about your past right now is because something at that women's shelter spooked you. From the moment you walked in, your back was ramrod straight. You not only looked uncomfortable with the gratitude offered by those women but you looked ill because of it. That concerned me then and it still concerns me now. Darla, whatever happened to you in the past caused those emotions to resurface tonight. *That's* what I care about because it's clearly affecting you right now, in the present.'

'So you want me to…what? Open up to you? Talk about my past?' She turned to face him but kept her arms folded as though she needed protection from his probing questions.

'You seem to be living by a code of silence that you've no doubt inflicted on yourself. Perhaps, tonight, it's time to break that silence. Talk about your past so whenever someone else says "Thank you", and believe me they will, you won't feel upset.'

Darla listened to his words, her heart wanting to tell him, wanting to trust him, wanting to let go of the secret shame she'd carried around for most her life. She rubbed her hands on her upper arms, trying to resist the urge to turn and walk away, to ignore him completely.

Could she tell him? Was he really sincere? The fact that he wasn't afraid of her, that he didn't kowtow to her, that he didn't hide from the truth, were good things. Surely she could break her rules just this once and open up to him? Her heart started to hammer against her chest, the blood thrumming in her ears, perspiration peppering her hands and her brow. Could she do this? Open up to someone? Could she trust?

She'd tried it before—three times with three different men—and each and every time she'd been let down. It didn't seem to matter whether she'd been a geeky, gangly teenager or a medical student or even a qualified professional, the men she'd trusted had let her down, breaking her heart and forcing her back into her cocoon once more.

Now here was Benedict. Waiting and watching. Not making a sound in case he scared her off. He was patient, he was kind and he didn't pretend to be something he wasn't. He hadn't returned from Tarparnii and demanded his job back. Instead he'd weighed up his options and decided the top job wasn't for him any more.

He'd remained true to himself. Surely that was a good sign? Surely that showed he was honourable?

Benedict stayed silent, watching her closely. He could see her internal struggle and he fervently hoped she'd power through it rather than retreating once more.

My mother was a drug addict. My mother was a drug addict. The words spun round and round in her head. That was all she'd need to say to him. Benedict was an incredibly smart man and he'd quickly connect the dots. *My mother was a drug addict. Come on, Darla. Say them.*

Benedict didn't speak but instead walked towards her, reaching out to place a hand reassuringly on her upper arm.

Darla flinched, but only slightly, at the gentle touch. It was nice and reassuring and what a normal man would do to a normal woman who had captured his interest.

Could she do this? Could she tell the truth to the man who'd called her funny and beautiful and intriguing? Was it possible she could break free from the chains that had bound her for far too many years? *My mother was a drug addict. My mother was a drug addict.*

'My mother was a drug addict.' There. Although the words had come out in a rush, they were out and she sighed with relief, the fear, the tension, the stigma that went along with such a declaration flowing from her.

'Thank you—for trusting me. That couldn't have been easy to say, Darla.' His words were soft, gentle, encompassing. He brushed a lock of hair out of her eyes and tucked it back behind her ear, caressing her cheek with his fingertips. His gaze dipped to her mouth, her neck, her ear and back to her mouth again. 'What you must have gone through.' He shook his head, looking into her eyes once more, seeing the pain she'd kept locked away and hidden for far too long.

'Those children...tonight...in that house.' She breathed in deeply and forced herself to slowly let it go. 'That was me. Before I started school, I'd been in many different foster-homes while my mum went into rehab and tried to get clean. When she completed the programme, they'd return me to her. I was the child who always wore second-hand clothes, who couldn't understand why other children didn't want to play with me. I was the one who suffered. I was the one who was shunted from here to there, who was locked away, pushed aside...discarded.' Her voice broke on the word and she silently berated herself for becoming so emotional. She closed her eyes for a second and was surprised when a tear broke free of its bonds and slid down her cheek.

Benedict tenderly brushed it away with his thumb and when she looked into his eyes she was flabbergasted to discover *his* eyes glistening with unshed tears...tears for her.

'Oh, Darla. What you must have gone through.'

Her heart was hammering wildly against her chest and she wasn't quite sure whether it was from talking openly about her past or due to Benedict's nearness. He was such a nice man. So caring. So accepting, or at least that was how he appeared.

Could she trust him? She'd opened up to him, told him the truth about her mother, and still he was here, looking at her as though she were the most beautiful woman on the face of this earth. Did he really think that? Was she really that beautiful? That intriguing? That funny?

She wanted to be. She desperately wanted to be and

as he continued to gently stroke her cheek, the heat from his touch sending shockwaves of pleasure through her, such as she'd never felt before, Darla couldn't control the burning need she had to do something reckless. She wanted, just for once, to be out of control, to lose herself, to forget about her past, her present and her future.

She wanted to *feel*. To be like every other normal woman. She wanted to know what it felt like to have the lips of a handsome man on hers. A man who wasn't trying to force himself onto her but who seemed willing to hang back, allowing her to make all the moves, to take her own time, to learn to trust.

Was it possible? Could she really trust him, not only with the truth of her past but with the emotions of her heart?

Swallowing over her dry throat and dipping her gaze to look from his deep blue eyes to his sexy lips, Darla knew she needed to simply *do* rather than rationalise and think. *Just do. Just do.* And before she could allow any other thought into her mind, she leaned forward and pressed her lips firmly to Benedict's.

CHAPTER SEVEN

BENEDICT wasn't at all sure how it had happened—but it had. As much as he wanted to fight it, Darla was an amazing woman who was somehow becoming important to him. Was it because of her caring and giving nature, her desire to help other women and their children, or was it simply because she'd taken the chance and trusted him?

Could he, in turn, now let himself trust her? She was so different from Carolina. Darla was the genuine article, not someone who lived a life of lies and deception. Darla didn't seek a crown for the work she undertook, she simply wanted to help, to make a real difference in the lives of those less fortunate, and that positive, almost obsessive desire had sprung from a place of pain, a place of tragedy, a place of personal knowledge.

She was quite a woman and the more he learned about her, the more he seemed to be unable to control this strange need to protect her. To ensure she didn't burn out, that her fuse wasn't extinguished in the dark and dangerous world she walked through every night, and as he focused on the way the sweetness from her lips was fuelling the raging fire deep within him, he found it even more difficult to keep the kiss light and testing rather than fierce and unresisting. Ever since they'd met, he'd wanted to know what it would be like to kiss Darla and now he was finding out just how mind-numbingly incredible it was.

As he kissed her plump mouth, Ben felt the hint of a deep-seated longing that had been denied for far too long. He wanted to slide his arms around her, to have her as close to him as possible whilst plundering the depths of her delicious mouth, but he sensed that taking things slowly was the only way to go.

This woman was special and as such she deserved to be cherished, to feel secure in the new emotions they were presently exploring. He had no real idea what she'd been through but even with the small part of her past she'd shared, he could well imagine how much pain she'd suffered at the hands of others.

This uncontrollable need to hold her, to gather her close, to protect her surged through him again but once more he forced himself to tread lightly, to focus on the smallest sensations and to dwell in them. He eased back and pressed a few butterfly kisses to her cheeks. The softness of her perfect skin blending with the saltiness of her tears made for a heady combination of desire mixed with determination.

There was no sound outside, no cars, no birds, no kids playing in the street. No clocks ticking inside or anything else to disturb this perfect moment. Nothing seemed to exist but the two of them and Darla wanted it to continue for ever, to lose herself in this one moment where nothing bad could ever touch her.

She closed her eyes and lifted her chin to allow him greater access to her. His soft petal-fresh kisses were sweet and tender and she swallowed over the tantalising need for more growing deep down within. How could

Benedict be so willing, so eager to kiss a blazing trail of delight from her cheek to her ear and down her neck? Why wasn't he repulsed by her declaration? Why hadn't he run a mile? Why was he still here, creating absolute havoc with her equilibrium?

Had she finally made the right decision? Confided in the right person? He'd said he wasn't interested in her past, that it didn't matter except where it had an impact on her present, and as he hadn't run screaming from the room, perhaps he'd really meant it. Was it possible for her to continue to confide in him? To continue to allow herself to feel this way for a man she barely knew? All she could think about at the moment was having his mouth pressed firmly to hers once more instead of enduring the sensual torture he was inflicting with his perfect little kisses.

Lacing her fingers through his hair, she urged his head upwards before instinctively seeking out his mouth, pressing hers firmly to his. The way he was making her feel, all warm and special and sexy, gave her the sensations of falling without knowing if there was a safety net below, waiting to catch her. She needed to take charge, to be in control of what was happening between them, because then she knew she wouldn't fall. Yes, she was attracted to Benedict. Yes, he was proving himself to be a man of worth, someone she could possibly draw closer to and, yes, she knew even in admitting that to herself, she might be in danger of releasing her tight grip on the reality she'd built around herself. If she took control now, if she kissed him as both of them longed to be connected, she'd feel much calmer.

Gently parting her lips, she pressed them to his. Benedict's answer was to groan with delight. Slipping her tongue out to tantalise his mouth had him winding his arms about her waist, drawing her as close as possible. Darla couldn't help but revel in just how perfectly he was responding to her cues, at how his intense reaction only seemed to fuel the powerful need deep within her, and for one split second she wasn't at all sure which one of them was really in control.

Need continued to build, to force its way to the surface, and as he held her close, his mouth still creating sweet havoc with her senses, she was amazed at the repressed desire she could sense within him. Here, in his arms, she could really forget everything. Her past, her present and her future. Being in Benedict's arms gave her the opportunity to live in bliss, where only the two of them existed…and nothing else.

When she opened her mouth even wider, desperate for more, desperate to search through these wild emotions she'd never really felt before, she was astonished when he eased away. The motion was only ever so slight but with her fingers still threaded through his thick, dark hair, she felt the imperceptible movement.

'Darla,' he murmured against her lips, but she wasn't having any of it. He'd managed to get her to open up, to trust him, to *feel*, and now he was trying to pull away, to break the bubble she'd created around them? He kissed her again, once, twice, but she could still feel him drawing away, his hand sliding down her back to rest at her waist. 'Easy. There's plenty of time, love.'

Love? She broke her mouth free from his, annoyed and angry that he'd pulled her back to reality. She'd been more than happy to live in a fantasy world, even if it was only for a short while. 'I am not your *love*. I'm nobody's love. Never have been, never will be.' The bitterness in her words surprised them both and within the next second she'd pushed right away from him and turned back to the window, hugging her arms close in an effort to combat the sudden coolness as well as to protect herself. The sounds of the world around them returned and she closed her eyes, the ticking of her kitchen clock much slower than her pounding heart rate. How dare he fluster her! How dare he kiss her with such intensity, such abandon and then take it away, as though he knew what was right for her!

'Darla.' Benedict took a step towards her.

'Don't.' Her word stopped him in the same way as being hit with a sledgehammer. 'I don't want to hear platitudes or explanations or anything. All right?'

Benedict stayed where he was and shoved his hands into his trouser pockets. 'Sure.' Was Darla trying to push him away? Keep him at bay? Had he got too close? When she'd started to deepen the kiss, he'd wanted nothing more than to follow her on that journey, but through some grain of logical thought still running around in his mind he'd also realised she might be trying to lose herself in a temporary embrace…and he'd suddenly realised that maybe he didn't want this thing between himself and Darla to be temporary at all.

He cared about her. Even as he stared at her standing at the window, her back to him, her entire posture screaming for him to leave her alone, he knew she'd somehow worked her way into his life and that alone should be scaring him witless. She wasn't Carolina. He knew that, he accepted that, but she was a woman who had a lot of things on her mind, things to sort out. Did he really want to get involved with her? To help her navigate the rocky waters through her past and into a new life? There was no doubt he was concerned for her, that he wanted to protect her, but was he equipped to do that?

She was definitely feisty. He'd give her that and at times she seemed to be drawing him close with one hand and then pushing him away with the other. Could he handle her mood swings? Would he be doing either of them any good? He'd only just managed to make some sense out of his own past problems. Was he ready to be there for Darla? Give himself to her completely without fear? No matter how much she pushed and pulled him in different directions?

Dragging in a calming breath and pushing his multitude of questions to the side, Benedict stooped and tidied up the remnants of their pizza meal, carrying the rubbish into her kitchen.

'Leave it,' she called, just wanting him to go. She'd made a big enough fool of herself and now all she wanted was to be left alone. She'd all but thrown herself at Benedict and then, when he'd refused her advances, she'd been left feeling betrayed and hurt. It wasn't a new sensation. She'd felt it before but she'd thought Benedict was different. He'd said she was beautiful. He'd said she was funny and intelligent. Surely with the way he'd caressed her cheek, with the way he'd spread little tiny kisses over her skin, that it meant he'd *wanted* her. Right?

'It's no trouble,' he returned. She heard him turn on the tap and wondered what on earth he was doing. It was strange to have someone else in her little home, let alone a man. 'Do you want a cup of tea?'

'No. Thank you,' she added belatedly. She may be annoyed and confused but that didn't give her any cause to be more rude to him than she'd already been.

'Mind if I have one?' He'd come back into the room and she turned to find him leaning against the doorjamb.

'Yes, I do.' Darla sighed and shoved her hands

through her hair, wishing she hadn't taken it out. She felt more in control when her hair was up, when she wore her power suits, when she had her armour on. 'I think it's best if you go. I'm tired and I want to get at least a few hours' sleep before I head out tonight.'

He nodded. 'What time are you planning on going?'

'About two o'clock.'

He nodded. 'Between two and five. That's when the most carnage seems to happen.'

'Yes.' She adjusted her arms, recrossing them firmly over her chest.

'Is that the way it was when you were growing up?' The question was soft.

Darla glared at him, trying to convey her annoyance at the mention of her past. 'Yes.' The word was tinged with impatience. If he persisted in pursuing this line of questioning then she'd *make* him leave.

Benedict straightened up, slowly walking towards her. 'It must have been so difficult, so confusing, so painful for you.'

Darla continued to glare, continued to mentally try to hold him at bay, but, unlike every other male she'd ever met, Benedict didn't seem to be picking up on her signals. When he placed his hands on her shoulders, her arms suddenly became like lead weights and dropped to her sides, the anger and frustration draining out of her.

'I'm very stubborn, Darla.' His tone was gentle and intimate but there was a hint of determination mixed in as well. 'My brothers say it's one of my worst and best traits. When I sink my teeth into something...' Before he could stop himself he bent his head and captured her lips in a startling kiss, his teeth gently nipping at her lower lip. Darla gasped with surprised delight and stared into his eyes as he straightened just as quickly. 'I don't let go.' His gaze dipped to encompass her slightly parted lips, fighting his natural urges, before meeting her wide brown eyes once again. 'I like you, Darla. *A lot*. I also respect you, both as a medical professional and a woman. I don't know what sort of relationships you've had with men in the past but I'm here to tell you that I'm different.'

Benedict brushed his fingers over her cheek. 'Something dynamic is happening between us. I have no idea what exactly and it's scary but it's happening, whether we like it or not.' He paused, his breath fanning out over her face, caressing her. She could feel his own uncertainty and remembered him saying he'd gone to Tarparnii after the break-up of a bad relationship. She swallowed, unable to move, unable to look away, unable to stop herself from wanting him.

'Moving forward, especially into uncharted waters, is a huge step,' he continued. 'And I don't want to stand still, Darla. I don't want to let what might be the best opportunity of my life pass me by because I was too afraid to try. I want to try, to move forward too.' He leaned down and she gasped, thinking he might kiss her once more, but instead he brought his lips near her ear and whispered softly, 'I hope you're ready to try too.'

With that, he straightened once more and lowered his hands before turning and walking to the door. He gave her one of those smiles that churned the already excitable butterflies in her stomach, making her knees go weak. 'Sleep sweet, fairy princess, and stay safe.' With a wink he disappeared, closing the door behind him.

Darla stood where she was, unable to move her legs, unable to think clearly. She raised a hand to her forehead and rubbed her eyes, not at all sure what was happening. Ever since Benedict had walked into A and E, he'd confounded her, turning her nice, neat and ordered world upside down and inside out.

When she closed her eyes, all she could see were images of Benedict, memories of the way he'd kissed her, held her, gazed into her eyes as though she was incredibly special. Opening her eyes, she shook her head. How on earth was she supposed to sleep now?

'Ambulance is on its way in,' Heather told Benedict as she put down the phone. He was sitting at the A and E nurses' station, writing up a set of case-notes.

'What have we got, Heather?'

'Darla.'

Benedict was instantly alert, turning his head sharply to give the nursing sister his undivided attention. '*Darla*? My Darla? What's wrong? What's happened? Is she all right?' He tried desperately to ignore the pounding of his heart as a million different scenarios of Darla hurt, bruised, battered and bleeding flooded through his mind.

'"*My* Darla"?' Heather's smile was wide and it was only then Benedict realised what he'd actually said. 'That's a very telling statement, Ben.'

He glanced quickly around them, wondering if anyone else had overheard Heather's comment. Thankfully, though, as it was almost five o'clock in the morning, there weren't as many staff around as during the day shift.

'It's fine,' Heather continued. 'I won't say a word, except that it's great to see you moving on with your life after Car—' She stopped. 'Well…anyway…' Heather looked down at the piece of paper and read from it. 'Darla's the one who called. She's in the ambulance with a patient, a woman in her late thirties. Suspected drug overdose.'

'That's not going to be easy for her,' he muttered, feeling his heart rate slowly returning to a more normal rhythm.

'Pardon?' Heather asked.

He shook his head. 'Nothing. ETA?'

Heather tipped her head to the side and listened, the sound of ambulance sirens drawing closer. 'Ah…that sounds like your Darla now, ex-boss.'

Benedict rolled his eyes as he stood. 'Very funny,' he remarked, and the two of them walked towards the ambulance receiving bay.

'How's it going?'

Benedict looked cautiously at Heather, a little unsure about what she meant. He didn't want to answer and say anything wrong that might upset Darla. They'd only shared a few kisses and whilst she had been all he could think about since it had happened, he wasn't ready for the entire A and E staff to be gossiping about his love life—again. Everyone in the hospital seemed to know what Carolina had done to him and he wasn't looking to be the centre of their water-cooler rumour-mill sessions any time soon. 'How's *what* going?' he checked.

'Working as deputy. You used to be the boss and now you're not. It can't be easy, coming back to your old department and answering to someone else.'

'Darla's a good administrator.' He shrugged. 'I'm more than happy for her to take the job.'

'Even when she's *your* Darla?'

They stood just inside the doors that led to the ambulance bay, waiting for the vehicle to turn into the hospital grounds. Benedict exhaled and pushed a hand through his hair. 'Listen, Heather, please don't—'

Heather grinned. 'It's fine, Ben. I won't say a word. I can't promise not to tease you a little now and then but...' She pretended to lock her lips and throw away the key. 'My lips are sealed,' she mumbled as the ambulance came to a stop.

'Thanks,' he replied as they headed outside.

'Benedict?' Darla said when he opened the rear doors. 'What are you doing here?'

'Covering for Matt because his kids are sick. What have we got?' he asked as they manoeuvred the stretcher from the ambulance into TR1.

'Tina, thirty-seven-year-old woman, ingested unknown substance. Found unconscious. Vitals aren't good.' As Darla continued to give her statistics, they transferred Tina onto the hospital barouche. The paramedics headed out with their stretcher and Heather started cutting away Tina's clothes. Benedict worked alongside Darla, not only doing all they could to stabilise their patient but also keeping a close eye on his boss. He could already hear the tension in her tone mixed with worry and frustration.

'Heart rate's dropping,' she called, checking the monitor.

'Get ready to intubate.'

'She's crashing. Charge defibrillators,' Darla returned.

On and on they worked. The atmosphere surrounding them was one of darkness and Benedict felt a sudden chill slide down his spine. It was a sensation he'd felt on many occasions over the years and he knew what it meant. He was surprised, though, when Darla took a quick look over her shoulder, as though she could feel it, too.

In the next instant a long beeping sound came from the ECG.

'She's in V-fib,' Heather announced, removing all the leads.

Darla immediately picked up the defibrillator paddles. 'Charge to one-sixty.'

'Charging,' Heather returned.

'Clear!'

Darla administered the shock and waited for what seemed like an eternity but in reality was only a few seconds. Benedict checked Tina's pulse.

'Nothing.'

'One-eighty,' she said, and waited for Heather's confirmation of the new setting before administering the second shock.

'Nothing,' Benedict said again, his gaze flicking between Darla and the patient.

'Charge to two hundred,' she said. She administered another shock.

'Darla, I'm sorry,' Benedict said after a moment, removing his fingers from Tina's carotid pulse.

'No. Epinephrine. Draw up—'

'No.' Benedict came around her and removed the paddles from her hands. 'Pupils are fixed and dilated. She's gone.'

'No. No. She can't die. She can't be gone.' Darla started cardiopulmonary resuscitation, her words eager and frantic. 'This is wrong. I'm supposed to save her. I'm supposed to do this. This is what I do. She can't die!'

Benedict quickly handed the paddles to Heather then placed his hands on Darla's shoulders, but she shrugged him off as she continued counting.

'Oxygen, *stat*.'

'Darla,' Benedict urged.

'No. This is not happening again,' Darla ground out. 'Come on. Come on, Tina.'

Benedict could do nothing else except put his arms around Darla's waist and physically lift her up and away from the body. 'It's over, Darla. I'm calling it.'

'No.' She twisted, trying to get free of his hold, but it was too much for her. She pummelled her fists against his chest. 'No.'

'Time of death, oh-five thirty-two.'

Darla was still upset, still lashing out at him, although he could feel the fight starting to drain out of her. He pulled her closer into his arms, stroking her back. 'You did everything you could.'

'No, I didn't.' Her body was starting to shake and he could feel she was crying. 'I *didn't*.' With that, she spun from his arms and stalked out of the room, leaving Heather and a few very startled nurses wondering what was wrong with their boss.

'Ben?' Heather queried.

Benedict turned to look at her. 'Are you all right here? Can you manage?'

'Er…yes, but—'

'Thanks.' With that, he headed out of the room, wanting to catch Darla before she completely disappeared. He walked into the main A and E corridor but there was no sign of her. Where could she possibly have disappeared to so quickly? It was then he heard a faint click, the sound of a door closing nearby, and he headed in the direction of her office. He swiped his pass-card through the lock opening the door into Syd's office. As he stood there, outside Darla's door, he could hear soft, muffled sounds coming from within. His heart turned over with empathy.

Without hesitation he swiped the pass-card through

the lock and slowly entered her office. The lights were off, the room still dark, even though outside the sun was just beginning to rise. Carefully, he made his way around to her desk, thinking she'd be sitting in her chair, but when he reached it, he found it empty. He listened and then realised the crying was coming from the far corner of the room.

With his eyesight now adjusting to the dark, he quickly made his way to where he could now see her sitting on the floor, hugging her knees close, her head buried as she sobbed.

'Oh, Darla,' he murmured, but it wasn't until he crouched next to her and touched her shoulder that she even realised he was in the room. She jumped almost half out of her skin.

'Leave me alone!'

'You don't mean that.' He sat down beside her and rubbed his hand gently on her back.

'Yes, I do. Just go.'

'No. This is not a good time for you to be alone, Darla. It's OK to lean on me.'

She shook her head and sniffed. 'No, it's not. I don't lean on anyone. I don't rely on anyone. I don't trust anyone. Only me. Only me.' Tears continued to stream down her face and Benedict quickly pulled a clean hand-kerchief from his pocket and pressed it into her hands.

'Not any more. I'm here. I'm not going anywhere.' Benedict continued to simply sit there, rubbing her back and offering all the support he could. He didn't tell her not to cry. He didn't tell her she was being foolish, over-reacting. He simply sat there while she cried and although she was perplexed at his behaviour, unable to understand why any man would want to sit beside a woman who was wailing like a banshee, she couldn't deny his presence made her feel infinitely better.

'I couldn't save her,' she said after a little while, her tears beginning to subside.

'You tried.'

'I didn't do enough.'

'You did everything you could.'

'I should have tried harder.'

Something in her tone, the vehemence, the anger, the frustration, tugged at his mind. Why did she feel so responsible for what had happened to Tina? If her mother had been an addict, surely she would have seen…

Benedict stopped rubbing her back for a moment and Darla slowly raised her head to look at him. It was when he looked into her eyes that he realised she wasn't talking about Tina. No. She was talking about her mother.

CHAPTER EIGHT

'Darla?'

'I couldn't save her.' She was looking at him but he could tell she wasn't seeing him. Her mind had slipped back into her past. He sat still, his hand resting on her back as he waited for her to talk.

'She'd overdosed before but each time I'd managed to call the ambulance in time.' She shook her head slightly. 'Not this time.' Darla's tone was soft and quiet, only invaded by the occasional hiccup as her tears began to dry.

'After school I'd gone to the library to do some more homework, trying desperately to get ahead. I'd sit in that library and I'd work hard, desperate to pull myself out of the cesspit that was my life. There weren't going to be any hand-outs, any miracles. I had to rely on myself and no one else. I was determined.' She sighed and closed her eyes.

'I came home from the library and I knew...I could just sense it. As soon as I opened the door something was...different. There was this sort of...presence in the apartment.' She screwed her eyes tight and shook her head as though wanting to rid her mind of the memory once and for all.

'Death. I'd never really smelt it or felt it before but this time it settled over me like a lead blanket, its rancid stench filling my lungs. I couldn't breathe properly and I started stumbling around the place, my heart racing as I searched frantically for her, alarm bells ringing in my ears.'

A lone tear slid down her cheek and Benedict only barely resisted the urge to wipe it away. Touching her, shifting, moving from exactly where he was might stop her from talking, from reliving a traumatic event from her past, which had clearly sculpted her life. He wondered if Darla had spoken to anyone about this before but even if she had, it would have been years ago.

'She was lying on the bathroom floor. Needle still in her arm. Eyes open. Pupils dilated. I ran to her. I called her name. Mum! *Mum!*' The urgency in her tone brought a lump to Benedict's throat, one he found would not shift no matter how many times he swallowed.

'I checked the pulse in her neck. It was faint but there. I took the needle from her arm and raced to the phone, only to find it wasn't connected. She hadn't paid the bill, again. I went next door and asked old Mrs Fowl to call an ambulance then raced back. I called to Mum, I slapped her face, grabbed a towel and wetted it with cold water and put it on her face.' Darla's words were fast, tripping over each other in her effort to explain the urgency. 'I made sure she was on her side, in the recovery position, so if she vomited, she wouldn't drown. I did everything I could. *Everything I could!*' She hiccupped again and shook her head. 'It wasn't enough.'

She opened her eyes and let the tears drop to her cheeks as she tried to blink them away. 'She arrested in the ambulance and they managed to revive her…but not for long. At the hospital, I stood in that treatment room. In the corner. Off to the side. Nobody saw me. They were all too busy doing what they could to save her.' She blinked, sniffed then raised her eyes to meet Benedict's for the first time since she'd started talking. 'It played out exactly as it did with Tina. The V-fib, the fixed and dilated pupils.' She shook her head again. 'I was sixteen and I stood in that treatment room and watched my mother die.'

Her tone was filled with complete desolation and despair and Benedict could take it no longer. He shifted around, settling himself firmly on the floor, leaning up against the wall before pulling Darla onto his lap and into his arms, holding her close. She didn't start crying again but she did put her arms around his neck, holding onto him so tight he hoped she'd never let go.

They sat like that for a while and then Darla shifted her face, leaning it more comfortably against his chest, listening to the steady rhythm of his heart. She couldn't believe how incredible it felt to have him hold her, to simply sit still and be. Never had she had this, feeling so secure and protected. It was her idea of heaven.

'Mum would always tell me,' she began softly, 'that I was a useless waste of space. Once, when she was drinking vodka and snorting cocaine, she told me she'd tried to have an abortion.' Darla cleared her throat and mimicked in a shriller pitch. '"Ya father was a loser. I'm a loser and you're a loser. I didn't want no baby and Runsie knew a doctor, he said, who could get rid of unwanted babies, but the idiot did it wrong and you were still there. Ya leech and you've been a leech since the day you was born."'

Benedict was shocked with what she was saying, anger towards her mother burning in his eyes, bile rising in his throat. He couldn't even speak, couldn't console her, he was so furious. Instead, he tightened his hold on her, wanting her to always feel safe with him.

'She only kept me around because the government paid child support. She'd use that money for her booze and drugs. How I lived through those first few years, I have no idea. I've been told I was in foster-care on and off for quite some time but they always sent me back to her. She was my mother and she would clean herself up just enough that they'd give me back—because that way she had her meal ticket again.

'At the age of seven she was sending me out to buy her drugs and if there were ever any raids around our neighbourhood, she'd hide her stash inside my tatty old teddy bear and make me hold it. "You scream your head off if the cops ever try to take it from you," she'd say. It worked every time and if I didn't scream loud enough, she'd pinch me when they weren't looking.'

As she continued talking, Benedict made a concentrated effort to relax his jaw because his head was really starting to pound with anger. 'Darla,' he murmured, unable to keep silent any longer. He rested his head against hers. 'I'm so sorry for what they did to you.' What she'd said also explained the drive she had for helping others who found themselves in similar situations to the one she'd grown up with. 'I wish I could help you. I want to take away the pain, to protect you from ever getting hurt again.'

Darla lifted her head and looked at him. 'You can't protect me, Benedict. Only I can.'

'Don't say that.'

'Why not? It's true. I've had to learn to fend for myself, to work hard, to make my own way in the world. At the age of sixteen, I was left all alone. No parents, no siblings, not even any friends, and yet I managed to stay under the government's radar, avoid being put into yet another foster-home and fend for myself. I studied hard, determined to get into medical school, working all sorts of jobs and taking out loans to pay for my tuition. I did it. By myself. With no help from anyone.'

Her tears and the emotions that had initially tipped her over the edge were starting to disappear and in their place appeared the strong, determined and incredibly stubborn woman who was starting to become more important to him than he'd dared to realise.

Darla shifted in his arms and he loosened his hold on her, not wanting her to feel hemmed in by his comforting embrace. She stayed where she was for another moment, as though she really did want to remain exactly where she was. He watched her internal struggle before she finally shifted off his lap and stood, walking over to her desk.

'Uh…thanks.'

'For?' Benedict asked as he levered himself upright and stretched his arms overhead to awaken stiff muscles. As he stretched, his shirt rose and the band of his denim jeans dipped, exposing a small section of his abdomen. Darla's gaze was unwittingly drawn to the movement, to the sight of his firm stomach muscles hidden beneath his clothes. Didn't the man have any idea just how crazy he could make her feel when he held her close, protected her whilst she blubbered all over his shirt and then excited her with the merest glimpse of his hard body hidden beneath his clothes?

When she didn't answer his question, he looked at her and was secretly delighted when he caught her staring at him. Darla had been ogling him. Surely this was a good sign, especially after the kisses they'd shared? She was still interested in him or, at least, he hoped so.

'Uh…for…um…you know…being supportive.' She momentarily closed her eyes against her stammering, unable to believe the way this man could fluster her so easily.

Benedict's slow smile spread across his lips, causing his eyes to twinkle. 'You are more than welcome.'

'No. Don't, Benedict.'

'Don't what?'

'Don't look at me like that.'

'Like what?'

'All cute and nice and gorgeous, especially when I'm embarrassed.'

'Embarrassed about what?' Darla's answer was to fix him with a look of incredulity. 'For crying? For getting upset? For opening up?' Benedict shook his head. 'Don't be.'

'I have to be.'

'Why?'

'Don't you have any idea what you do to me?' Darla placed both hands on her blotter and he could see she was struggling to find some semblance of calm. 'Where I was raised, men only ever wanted one thing from a woman and even then they took it rather than waiting for it to be given.'

Benedict's eyes widened at this news. 'Darla. Has a man ever—?'

'No,' she quickly answered. 'Well…almost once but thankfully my mother hit him over the head with a frying pan.'

'How old were you?'

'Thirteen.' She crossed her arms in front of her and rubbed her upper arms. Benedict wanted desperately to take her in his arms again, to hold her, to protect her, but he could also read the 'Keep Out' sign she'd erected and knew, if he was to continue earning her trust, he'd have to respect that.

'After that, my mother took to locking me in my room, especially when she had a guy coming around. "It's for your own protection," she'd say, and then hide the key.' Darla shook her head. 'One time I was locked in there for two days because she was so high on drugs she'd forgotten to unlock the door and let me out.'

Benedict's heart wrenched with pain at her words and he clenched his hands at his sides, determined to respect her wishes and keep his distance. It couldn't be easy for her to confess such things to him but he appreciated this sliver of trust she was giving him.

'The next time she was passed out I found the key, stole some of her drug money and went to the shops and had a key cut.'

'Smart.'

'That's right. I had to learn to be smart, to out-thwart her and all the deadbeats who would hang around our place. Any money I found lying around I'd steal and when I had enough saved up, I'd buy food. I grew up quickly. I did the shopping, I tidied the house, I learned self-defence. I had to clothe myself in mental bulletproof armour if I was going to survive, and I did.

'I may not have had a mother who loved me but because of her I did what needed to be done. No one else was going to do it. It was up to me.' She paused for a second, then angled her head to the side. 'Although I have to say, the day I truly understood that my mother didn't love me was perhaps the worst day ever. All children want to be loved, and in the beginning that's why I did whatever she told me to do. I wanted to win her approval. Then one day, about six months after the incident where she'd hit the man with the frying pan, I began to understand that she hadn't done that to *protect* me, she'd knocked him out because she was *jealous* of me.

My body was maturing, it was young, untouched, and hers was the complete opposite. She locked me away because she couldn't stand the thought of her lovers wanting *me* when they should have been wanting her.'

Darla couldn't believe that tears were once more pricking behind her eyes. Hadn't she cried them all out yet? She swallowed over the lump in her throat and worked hard to ignore the heaviness of her heart. 'She didn't love me. My mother didn't love me. She *never* loved me. She kept me around because I made her life easier. She was paid money from the government, I cooked and cleaned. I ensured she had clean clothes to wear, food to eat and a roof over our heads. All she cared about was herself, and once I'd managed to get that through my thick skull I started pulling those walls around me, hiding inside them, and they provided protection from outside attacks. I was safe so long as I relied on myself and no one else. It's why I prefer being an A and E doctor, why I go out onto the streets. I want to help people as no one ever helped me. They can at least have their angel to cling to. I had no one.' Her voice cracked on the last words and she quickly shook her head and cleared her throat.

'You do now.'

'What?'

'You have someone now. You have me.' Benedict edged forward, coming to stand right in front of her desk, but didn't make any move to touch her. 'I believe in you, Darla. I believe in the work you're doing, both on the streets and here at the hospital. You're a remarkable woman, like no one I've ever met before, and I completely admire you, but don't for one further second think you are alone. Not any more.' Benedict raked his hand through his hair and looked down at her.

'I don't have a clue what you've done to me, Darla, how you've managed to draw me in with your natural charm and intelligence, but you have. I've tried to fight it but I can't any more. And I know you may think my words are shallow, that my head is easily turned by a pretty face, that I'm as typical as every other male in the world, but I'm not. I wasn't looking for this attraction either. The last thing I wanted was to be involved with *anyone.* But it's there and I'm not about to ignore it.' He looked straight into her big brown eyes to ensure what he was about to say rang as true as possible because he meant every word.

'However, given what you've just shared, I want you to know you have nothing to fear from me. I want you to believe I'm someone you *can* trust and someone who *values* you. I won't rush you, Darla. I want to spend time with you, for us to keep discovering each other, to be open and honest, to celebrate and commiserate together. I will hold your hand, gaze longingly into your eyes, and be bowled over by your smile, but I will also be a polite and courteous gentleman at all times.' He placed his right hand over his heart. 'And that's a promise.'

Darla tried not to tremble at his words, at the way his rich deep tones washed over her, calming her, filling her with hope. Was this for real? Was it possible that she might actually have found a man who was genuine, honest and true? She'd opened up to him a lot and that in itself showed her he was worthy of at least trying to earn her trust. He'd held her when she'd cried. He'd offered comfort and support and the way he'd made her feel when she'd been safely cocooned in his protective embrace had been heavenly. Still, the battle between head and heart continued to war within her and she nodded once at his words before straightening her shoulders and lifting her chin.

'Don't promise, Benedict. Prove it.'

A slow smile spread over his face, lighting his eyes and melting her heart. 'I intend to.'

Benedict held her gaze and she could see he was completely serious. It was intense and powerful and the emotions coursing through her made Darla feel exposed, vulnerable. She didn't like it but at the same time she was almost desperate to once again experience the warmth of his arms about her. Throughout her life she'd learned to rely solely on herself, not wanting anyone to see her vulnerability. Yet not more than five minutes ago she'd been sitting on Benedict's lap, with his arms firmly around her as she'd talked of her past. Even now, as her gaze flickered over him, she could see wet patches on his shirt where her tears had fallen.

She wanted desperately to trust him, to believe what he'd said was true, and now she'd challenged him to prove it. Had she gone completely insane? She looked away from his hypnotic eyes, focusing on the new files Syd had put into her in-box. She went to gather them up and then noticed the little red light flashing on her telephone, indicating she had a voice message. That was odd. It was a Saturday morning and usually, if there was an emergency, she'd be contacted on her cellphone. It didn't matter that today was officially her day off as she'd planned to come in anyway and get a jump start on some paperwork.

'Leave the files,' Benedict said, watching her every move. 'It's Saturday. You're not rostered on. You've had an emotionally draining night and morning and you've been taking enough files home to sink a battleship.'

'There's a message,' Darla said, pointing to the phone,

and quickly picked up the receiver, pressing the button to replay the message.

'All right, but after that I'm taking you ho—'

'Shh.' Darla held up her hand and Benedict noticed her eyes start to widen as she listened. The message was obviously short as it wasn't a moment later that she replaced the receiver and sat down in her chair.

'Well? What was it?' he asked when she didn't speak. He walked around the desk to come stand beside her chair. 'Darla?'

'I got the job.'

'That's fantastic. I always knew you would. Congratulations!'

'I got the job.' She uttered the words as though she was in complete shock. 'This time I did it.' She shrugged, the reality of her situation still sinking in. 'I really did it.'

'This time?' he queried as he leaned against the desk, legs out long, hands on the table beside him.

Darla closed her eyes as though savouring the moment. 'Before I came here, I was in Sydney, working at A and E at Sydney General. I was acting director there and had a very good chance of getting the directorship.' She opened her eyes and looked at him. 'One of my colleagues, Colin, was also going for the job. We'd been colleagues for years, built up a healthy competition, and I'd thought he was someone I could perhaps one day come to trust—I mean *really* trust.'

'Like you trust me?' He couldn't help giving her a playful wink and was rewarded with a half-smile.

'Shut up,' she returned gently, before standing up and walking over to the fern in the corner of her office. She reached out and touched the green leaves.

'Anyway, after years of working together, of spending our free time together, of him declaring he wanted our friendship to evolve into something more, something real, something romantic...' she dropped her hand and turned to face Benedict '...he stabbed me in the back.'

'What happened?' Benedict stayed where he was, resisting the urge to haul her into his arms.

'Well, the fact that we'd both applied for the same job was starting to cause tension between us. Colin suggested that we both withdraw and allow someone else to take the job, thereby choosing our relationship over work. One other person from a hospital in Brisbane had also applied for the job and after much discussion we decided to let it go. That our relationship was more important than a job.'

'Let me guess, Colin didn't withdraw his application?'

'Got it in one. Afterwards, he was confused as to why we couldn't continue with our relationship, why I didn't want anything to do with him.'

Benedict nodded as though all those times she'd asked him whether he really wanted the top job finally made sense. She'd thought he'd been going to change his mind. 'He'd lied to you.'

'Just like every other man in my life. Foster-fathers, social workers, drug dealers, boys at school, men at medical school, professional colleagues. They always want something, Benedict. Always.' She started to pace back and forth. 'In high school, about a year before my mother died, there was this new guy who came to the school and we hit it off straight away. He was smart, like me. We would both hide in the library at lunchtime, studying, reading, keeping out of the way of playground ridicule. I was young, naive and thought perhaps here was someone I could trust, but after a while he started

coming less and less to the library. He started changing, fitting in with the "cool" crowd, and by the end of
the year he'd completely snubbed me.'

'But teenage boys are like that, Darla. They're fickle
and filled with raging hormones. You shouldn't take it
personally.'

'Oh, no? Well, at one stage I confronted him. Asked
him why he didn't seem to want to be my friend any
more, and he told me he didn't hang around with drug
addicts.'

'What?'

'Yep. He'd listened to the gossips. Listened to the ru-
mours flying around about me instead of coming to me
and asking me directly. So that was lesson one. Lesson
two didn't happen until my final year of medical school
when I once again let down my guard and started dating
a fellow student. I'd told myself I was different now. My
mother had been dead for years, I'd managed to work
hard, to get into medical school, and I was doing very
well. I was a different person now and I could handle the
opposite sex.' She shook her head. 'He was a charmer.
So much so that he ended up dating three girls—at once.
When the other two found out, they didn't seem to care,
but for me—'

'He'd broken your trust.'

'He'd lied to me and used me. It was the same pattern
I'd seen with all men over time.' She stopped pacing
and stood in the middle of her office, her arms spread
wide. 'So you can see, Benedict, why I can't simply take
you at your word. You say I'm different. You say I'm
remarkable, that I'm worth it. You say that you won't
rush me, that I can trust you, and that's why I need you
to prove it.'

'I need to pay for every other man's sins,' he stated, wanting to show her he understood.

'Yes.'

'I accept that challenge, fairy princess, and we'll start right now.' He walked over and took her hand gently in his. 'Come on.'

'Wait.' She pulled her hand free. 'What are you doing?'

'I'm taking you out to celebrate.'

'Celebrate?'

'Darla! You just got the job of your dreams. This needs a celebration. A *big* celebration.'

'And I suppose you have something in mind?' She placed her hands on her hips and glared at him.

'I do.' He stepped closer, leaning down to whisper in her ear. Darla closed her eyes, forcing herself to ignore the spicy scent of him, ignore the comforting warmth emanating from him, ignore the way she wanted to turn her head to ensure their lips met. 'The best celebration ever,' he continued, his breath fanning her neck. 'Apple pie.'

'What?' She pulled back. 'Is that your new romantic nickname for me or—?'

Benedict laughed and the sound warmed her through and through. 'Darla, you're never boring, I'll give you that. No, I mean let's go celebrate with the best apple pie you've ever eaten.' This time he held out his hand and waited ever so patiently for her to put her hand in his. She looked at her desk, at the work sitting there, then she looked at his face, then back to his hand.

'You deserve this. You deserve to celebrate. This is big news, Darla, and it requires a big celebration in return.'

'Apple pie is a big celebration?'

His only answer was a slow, soft nodding of his head. 'Come on,' he urged. 'We have to start somewhere.'

He was right. She'd already let down her guard, not only telling him about her past, her mother and the men who had previously broken her trust but showing him just how vulnerable she really was beneath the hard protective layers she'd pulled around her over the years... and he hadn't done an about-face and run away.

She had to start somewhere. Benedict was a good man. He'd listened, he'd been patient, he hadn't pressured her. Could she take the chance? Take a step forward into a world she'd only dreamt about? A world where she was a normal woman, with a normal job and a normal boyfriend? *We* have to start somewhere. He was in this with her. He was taking a chance as well, putting himself back out there after a bad relationship. Could she prove to Benedict that he could trust her too? Risk his heart once more?

'OK' came her tentative reply as she placed her hand in his. 'Pie it is.'

CHAPTER NINE

AT THE end of his shift, they took a taxi back to where Darla had parked her car.

'Haven't you got a car yet?' she asked, rolling her eyes when he shook his head. 'OK. Where's this great pie place?'

'Uh…why don't you go home, shower first, get all refreshed before celebrating?'

She seemed mildly relieved. 'Really?'

'Of course.' He opened the driver's door for her. 'I'll come pick you up in…' He looked at his watch. It was almost eight o'clock in the morning. He did a few quick mental calculations. 'About forty-five minutes? Sound good?' Darla nodded and Benedict leaned forward and pressed a quick kiss to her cheek. 'OK. I'll see you then.' He waited for her to climb behind the wheel and then shut the door. She quickly rolled down the window.

'What are you going to do?'

'Uh…I'll go shower and change, too.'

'I can drop you at your house. According to your personnel file, you don't live far from my place.'

'Thanks, but it's fine. I have a few other things to organise,' he returned.

'Like what?'

'Like how I'm supposed to surprise my girlfriend

when she keeps asking questions?' He shook his head but his smile was bright. 'Go home. See you in just under an hour.' And with a wink he turned and started jogging down the street, leaving Darla sitting in her car, stunned.

'Girlfriend?'

Forty-six minutes later, Benedict rang her doorbell and Darla, fresh from her shower and dressed in a comfortable pair of jeans, boots and a pale blue shirt, answered the door. Her hair wasn't completely dry so she'd left it loose and Benedict simply stood on the other side of the threshold, struck dumb at the sight of her.

'Aren't you going to come in?' she asked, stepping back to allow him access.

'You look beautiful.' He closed his eyes for a moment as though needing to steel himself before looking at her again. 'This chivalry thing is going to be harder than I thought,' he muttered, but she heard and couldn't stop the bubble of delight that zipped through her.

'Good,' she replied, and as he still hadn't moved she swept her arm in front of her. 'You're not coming in?'

'Uh…' Benedict shoved both hands into his pockets to stop himself from reaching out to touch her, to draw her close to him, to kiss her gorgeous mouth. 'I don't mind waiting in the car. It might be safer, at least until I can get my hormones under control,' he replied with a sheepish grin.

'Oh.' Darla was surprised to find her cheeks feeling warm at his words. He really did think she was beautiful. She could see it in his eyes and the knowledge made her feel incredibly special. 'OK, then. I'll get you the keys.'

'No. I meant my car.' He jerked a thumb over his shoulder.

'You mean Hamilton's car?'

'No. Mine. I just went and bought one.'

'What?'

'I bought one,' he repeated. 'Go. Get ready. I'll be waiting.' He turned and walked towards the white sedan parked in her driveway. Darla leaned out the door and realised he was telling the truth. He'd just gone out and bought a car! Stunned, she quickly made sure all her windows were locked and picked up her bag and jacket before slipping her sunglasses on and heading out.

When Benedict saw her, he quickly came around to the passenger door and opened it for her.

'Thank you.'

He winked. 'Chivalry, right?'

Her answer was a brilliant smile as she settled herself in the car. Benedict came around to the driver's side and climbed in, both of them buckling their seat belts before he started the engine. 'Sounds great,' she said.

'Do you know much about cars?' he asked as he reversed.

'No. Not really.'

'Neither do I. So long as they get me from A to B without breaking down, I'm happy.'

She laughed then asked, 'So where's this secret apple-pie shop?'

'Actually, it's a bit of a drive but as neither of us are rostered on today and as we're celebrating, I thought a drive would be nice.'

Darla could feel her apprehension starting to increase at this change in events. She wasn't a big fan of surprises but had to remind herself that she was stepping into the unknown. The way Benedict made her feel, all happy, mixed up and delightedly confused, was a good thing. She'd opened up to him in a way she'd never thought she could open to *anyone*. Perhaps she should try something new? Follow his lead.

'Are you all right with that?' he asked when she didn't say anything. 'Because if you're not, if you're not ready for surprises, then we can make other plans.'

'No.' She turned to face him.

'Er…no, you're not all right or…?'

'Don't make other plans. It's good for me to…step outside my very comfortable comfort zone.'

Benedict's smile was bright at her words and he reached over and took her hand in his, bringing it to his lips to kiss it. 'It really is the best pie I've ever tasted.'

'Then my life, and my gastronomic delight, are in your capable hands.' Darla settled her head back against the headrest and sighed, feeling a contentment like she'd never felt before.

Benedict slowed the car as they neared the town of Batlow where the apples were grown, cooked and made into the best pie in the country. He glanced across at Darla, and smiled at the sight of her sleeping peacefully in the seat beside him. They'd made it to the motorway, heading out of Canberra towards Tumut, which was the small town where he'd gone to school, before exhaustion had claimed her. She'd slept soundly for over an hour and now as he decreased speed yet again she began to stir.

'Hello,' he murmured as he brought the car to a stop, parking on the side of the road near the memorial park. Darla gazed at him, her eyes still fuzzy.

'Hi.' She smiled.

'You've had a good sleep.'

At his words Darla suddenly realised where she was.

She shifted so quickly in her seat that the seat belt restrained her. 'What? Where are we?' She looked around, remembering she was in a car, a car with Benedict, a car she'd fallen asleep in. She closed her eyes as mortification washed over her.

'We're in Batlow and, by the looks of things, it's going to be a great turnout.'

'What?' She opened her eyes and looked at the view outside the windows. There were people all around, quite a lot of people actually, and cars seemed to be parked everywhere. There were families and children and laughter and sunshine and happiness and…normalcy.

'Benedict, I fell asleep!'

'I know. I was there.'

'But…you shouldn't have let me.'

'Why not? You were obviously exhausted.'

'But I don't—' She stopped as the words she wanted to say would sound ridiculous on her tongue.

'Don't what?' he prompted as he unclipped both their seat belts.

'I don't…sleep in front of people.'

'Oh. Well, it's just as well I'm not people.' With a wide grin he exited the car and quickly came around to her side, opening the door for her. 'You might need your jacket. It's a little cooler here than in Canberra.'

Pushing aside her embarrassment, Darla gathered up her handbag and jacket before allowing him to help her from the car. 'The last thing I remember was setting your radio stations,' she murmured.

'And you found one that played nice soothing jazz. So soothing you dozed off.' He shrugged. 'You've nothing to be worried about, Darla.' His words were light, fresh and held a hint of teasing. 'You didn't snore.'

She opened her eyes wide, glaring at him, but he only

laughed in response and took her hand in his. 'Come on. Lots to do and explore and pie to eat.'

'What *is* this? I thought we were going to a little café somewhere.'

'I like to be original for first dates.'

'This is a date?'

'No. This is the Batlow annual *apple* pie fair. The *date* fair isn't held until October.'

'Really?'

'No. I'm making it up. Come on. I'm hungry.'

She wasn't sure why but she allowed him to lead her towards the showgrounds where there were stalls and tables and chairs and music and laughter. She was also surprised at the number of people who seemed to greet Benedict as though they were old friends.

'Oh, you came, you came, you came!' A woman with long honey-coloured hair came running up to Benedict, her arms out wide. Benedict instantly dropped Darla's hand and caught the woman in a fierce hug, even spinning her round. Once her feet were firmly back on the ground, she planted a big kiss on his cheek. 'I'm so happy to see you. You look great.'

Darla stared at the woman and started to wonder whether there was more going on here than Benedict had let on. Who was she? Why had she greeted him in such a familiar fashion? Wasn't she a bit old to be twirled around like a child?

'Thanks. It's good to see you, too. It's been too long.'

The woman gave his arm a playful nudge. 'Over twelve months. Still, you're back.'

'I am.' Benedict placed his hand in the small of Darla's back. 'Darla, I'd like you to meet my exuberant sister-in-law, Honeysuckle.'

Darla released a breath she hadn't realised she'd been

holding and smiled at Benedict's sister-in-law. This woman was family and she already knew how important family was to Benedict. She held out her hand. 'Pleased to meet you.'

'Oh, we don't bother with that here,' Honey remarked, waving Darla's hand away and pulling her close into a warm embrace. Darla stared at Benedict over Honey's shoulder, her eyes wide. Benedict's reply to her unspoken question was to shrug as though to say 'That's Honey'.

'Where's Edward?' Benedict asked, looking around for his brother.

Honey released Darla. 'Over at the face-painting stand with the children, although we all know it's going to be washed off with the apple bobbing later today but it's all in good fun.' Her exuberance was like nothing Darla had seen before.

'And the baby?' Benedict continued as they walked slowly towards the face-painting stand. 'Where's my beautiful new niece?'

'Eddie has her in the papoose. I've been here since before sunrise, baking pies, so I can guarantee they're fresh. Oh, hey…' Honey was distracted by someone else and waved wildly. 'Sorry. Need to keep going. Next year I've promised Eddie I *won't* be on the organising committee.'

'Sure, sure,' Benedict joked. 'I've heard that one before, Hon.'

She grinned at him before looking to Darla. 'It was great to meet you,' she replied. 'I'll catch up with you both later.' And as fast as she'd come, she was off, absorbed in the crowd of people milling their way between stalls.

'So…I take it you live around here?'

Benedict nodded. 'Oodnaminaby's about half an hour from here by the main roads but twenty on the back roads, but you can only drive them in the warmer months. In winter, they're closed due to the snow.'

'This is the first time you've been back since returning from Tarparnii?'

'Yes.'

'Why didn't you mention this?'

'Because it's part of your celebration surprise.'

'To introduce me to your family?'

He shrugged and slipped his hand back into hers, realising the enormity of her question. 'That's a by-product. Truly, Darla. You'll love the apple pies, and then, if you want, I'll even pay for you to have your face painted.'

Darla stared up at him as though he'd gone completely bonkers but she found his eyes alive with life, his smile wide with happiness, and both of them were highly infectious. 'You're crazy,' she said with a little laugh.

Benedict nodded. 'Better you find out now.' With that, he steered her towards the pie stands, where they joined one of the long queues. Finally, they were sitting at a table, about to have their first tasting of pie.

'Wait.' Benedict stopped her and held his fork up in the air. 'A toast.'

'With forks?'

'Why not?' He cleared his throat. 'Congratulations on your new job, *Director* Fairlie. You deserve it.'

'Thank you,' she responded, and grinned when he tapped his fork against hers, then started eating his pie. He closed his eyes and savoured the delight. Darla took her first bite.

'Was I right, or was I right?' he asked and Darla swallowed her mouthful, nodding.

'It's…delicious.'

'It's *heavenly*,' he said, and she laughed.

'This is lovely, Benedict. A great idea for a celebration even if it wasn't what I was initially expecting.'

'Surprise,' he said softly, and reached across the table to take her hand in his. He laced their fingers together and smiled at her. 'Thanks for letting me in, Darla. I know it hasn't been easy but I appreciate it.'

Darla stared across the table at him, her gaze dipping from his eyes to his lips. She wanted him to lean across, to capture her mouth in one of the glorious kisses they'd shared before…but he didn't. Instead he winked and smiled and she could see he was using incredible restraint. He had to learn to trust completely again too. He'd promised not to rush her, to let her set the pace for the romantic emotions surging between them, proving that he was definitely someone she could come to trust.

Hours later, after a day of looking at the different craft stalls, laughing as people actually bobbed for apples in large barrels of water and seeing Benedict give shoulder rides to a few of his nieces and nephews, Darla was starting to feel rather exhausted. Honey had invited them back for dinner and although Darla wanted to start the journey back to Canberra fairly soon, she was also curious to see the home where Benedict had grown up.

'At least have a good meal before you head off,' Honey had said. 'Or you're more than welcome to stay the night if you choose. We're in no hurry for you to rush off,' she'd remarked, her gaze encompassing both of them. 'After all, Ben, it's still your family home.'

'Do you want to go?' he'd asked Darla, even though she could see quite clearly that he would love to have a few more hours with his siblings. During the day, and between bites of apple pie, she'd been introduced to Peter and his wife Annabelle and their two boys, as well as to Benedict's surrogate sister Lorelai and her husband Woody and their two girls. It had been interesting to meet Peter and Edward, noting the clear genetic heritage the three brothers shared. Dark hair and blue eyes were the order of the day yet all of them possessed their own unique qualities.

'Of course. I'd love to stay for dinner. After all, this is my celebration day.'

His eyes had twinkled with delight and his mouth had beamed into a bright smile. 'Yes, it is.' Then he'd surprised her by bowing from the waist. 'Thank you, Darla.'

The Goldmark house in Oodnaminaby was what Darla had always pictured as the perfect family home. Two storeys, filled with photographs and pictures and toys and people and kids intermingling everywhere. Honey and Edward's latest addition to the clan, three-month-old Susan, was cradled securely in Benedict's arms.

'How are you holding up?' he asked Darla as Susan gurgled up at him, safe and secure in the knowledge she was loved unconditionally.

'It's…loud,' she said, and he smiled.

'We do tend to get a bit rowdy. It's even worse with Bart and Ham here.'

'Do you get together often?'

He nodded. 'A few times a year at least. Special occasions, Christmas, New Year.' He shrugged. 'It all depends on shifts.'

A loud clanging sound came from the kitchen and Susan jumped in his arms. A moment later a frown furrowed her cute little brow and he could tell she was about to start crying. 'Why don't we go out into the garden?' He looked at Darla. 'Care to join Susan and me for a pre-dinner stroll?' He cradled Susan carefully in one arm and offered the other to Darla.

'I'd love to,' she said as she slipped her hand into the crook of his elbow. They slipped through the kitchen and out the back door, heading towards the back garden. There was a small building to one side and opposite it the most beautiful little garden Darla had ever seen.

'That's the old coach house,' he remarked, indicating the building. 'It took my father years to restore. My mother would complain that it was taking him too long and he'd say, "Well, I can only work on it in my spare time so if you want it finished sooner, roster me some more spare time."' Benedict smiled as he recalled his father's words. 'They worked together, they raised a family together and they died together, and they did it all with love.' He studied the building for a moment before turning and walking down the few steps of a small neatly trimmed garden. There were pretty flowers on one side and native shrubs on the other and in the dimming light Darla saw a small stone bench with words engraved on it.

'"Hannah and Cameron",' she read out loud.

'This was my mum's garden. Her sanctuary where she could come and have five minutes' peace. She designed and planted it but over the years, whenever we had something to discuss with her, or a problem we couldn't solve, she'd bring us out into the garden, get us doing some weeding and then just as she'd gently pull the weeds from the ground, she'd pull the weeds from our lives.' Benedict stood, looking out at the setting sun. Darla sat down on the bench and watched him. Little

Susan had stopped fussing and had closed her eyes, quite content with the world.

'Do you miss her?' The question was soft.

'Yeah. Probably more than I miss my dad. She was busy. What woman wouldn't be with five boys, a husband and a busy country practice? But she always made time for us. Each and every one. No matter what. She'd sit on the grass and she'd pull weeds, waiting patiently for us to talk out whatever was on our minds.'

'So if she was here now,' Darla asked, knowing she was branching into uncharted waters but unable to stop herself, 'what would you say?'

Benedict smiled. 'I'd tell her all about you. About how you work too hard. How you help restore people's hope when they think that it's gone for ever. I'd tell her about how you make me laugh, about the way your whole face lights up when you're happy. I'd tell her how you've managed to restore my faith in the opposite sex by proving you're a woman of worth.'

'Why was your faith broken, Benedict? What happened to make you go to Tarparnii?'

'You mean you haven't heard the hospital gossip?'

'I don't listen to it.'

'Of course you don't. See, Susan?' he said to his niece. 'A woman of worth.' Benedict looked at Darla and exhaled slowly. Now was the time to tell her everything and put the past to rest. 'Her name was Carolina and, quite frankly, she lied and deceived me at every turn. We'd known each other for a few years but after a while our friendship started to become more personal, but as it turns out, Carolina wasn't really interested in *me*. The only reason I'd made her radar was because I'd been promoted to A and E director. She was a gold-digger, latching onto me in the hope that I'd give her everything she wanted. She pretended to be someone she wasn't. She would tell me what a great nurse she was and how she'd really helped a lot of her patients with their emotional issues. She built herself up to be so great, I believed her. She even started volunteering with ACT NOW, always telling me how much she really wanted to help the homeless... But it was all false. All she wanted was my signature to open a joint bank account before she could clean me out. We'd even started looking at homes to buy and I'd planned on asking her to marry me.'

'So what happened to break the spell? To open your eyes?'

'One night, at ACT NOW, there was a riot. I mean, a really bad one, and the rioters turned their attention onto us. They were outside the ACT NOW vans and started rocking the medical van to and fro, with both Carolina and myself inside. The van was tipped and Carolina sustained a fracture to her clavicle, humerus, ulna and tibia, as well as a mild concussion. Basically, she was so mad at me, mad that because of me, because she'd been pretending to like that sort of work, she'd been injured.'

'The rose-coloured glasses came off?'

'Smashed to smithereens,' he agreed. 'I couldn't believe it. The woman I'd thought I loved wasn't real. She was fictitious and not only that, she was deceitful. She was in hospital for a week because of the concussion and she blamed me for her injuries. She even threatened to sue me, but none of it was my fault so she really didn't have a leg to stand on—literally.'

'So you went to Tarparnii?'

'Not straight away. At first I threw myself into my work, becoming demanding and critical of my staff. I was hurt, bitter, and alienated quite a few people. I avoided coming home because I knew Edward would no doubt lecture me on my behaviour and he would have been right, too. Then, when I finally did come home, exhausted and burnt out, Edward didn't say a thing. Instead, he unleashed his secret weapon.'

'What's that?'

'Honeysuckle *and* Lorelai. The two women in the world I knew I could trust. Lorelai was twenty when my mum died and while she was good at supporting and caring, it was Honey who could really pull those weeds the way Mum used to. Between the two of them I didn't stand a chance. Honey suggested Tarparnii and within two weeks I'd applied and been granted a sabbatical and was on a plane heading overseas.'

He came and sat down next to her on the bench seat, carefully shifting a sleeping Susan to his other arm.

'I'm sorry you were hurt,' Darla said softly.

'More my pride than anything. Turns out she didn't do as much permanent damage as I'd originally thought.'

'That's good news.'

'Is it?' Benedict shifted and looked at her, their faces close. His gaze dipped to look at her lips and even though the light was fading fast, he could still see every contour of her beautiful face, simply because he'd memorised it.

'Yes.'

'Darla, I want to kiss you.'

'I'm right here,' she murmured, feeling his glorious warmth surround her, feeling her heart hammering wildly against her ribs due to his nearness, feeling light-headed and ready to take a chance.

'I know. Your senses are drugging me, enticing me, urging me forward...' He leaned closer, gazing at her parted lips, their breath mingling with delight. 'But I can't.'

'You can't?' She was unable to hide the hint of desperation in her tone.

'I promised. I want you to trust me, Darla. It's even more important to me now than it was this morning and I'm not going to break that trust, even if it drives me slowly around the twist.'

CHAPTER TEN

IT WAS almost midnight when Benedict pulled up out-side Darla's apartment and once again she was sleeping soundly in the seat next to him. Even when he switched off the engine, she still remained asleep, indicating just how exhausted she was.

He was fairly sure she was planning to head out to the streets at two o'clock in the morning, even though she'd probably do herself more good by actually getting one good night's sleep. Working all day and then being the angel every night would soon take its toll on her and he didn't want her collapsing from exhaustion, which was where he could see she was heading. At least he'd man-aged to get her away from the constant grind today. He smiled as he recalled the way she'd interacted with his family. She'd been shy and reserved at first but during dinner she'd slowly started to come out of her shell.

She'd offered to stack the dishwasher and tidy the kitchen with Edward whilst Benedict had helped Honey with the bedtime routine. Lorelai, Woody and their two girls had left first, with Peter and Annabelle staying around a bit longer as their two boys were older.

'They're all so wonderful,' she'd told him as they'd waved goodbye to start the two-hour drive back to Canberra.

'I'm glad you like them.'

'I do. I'd always dreamed of a family like that but I never thought I'd get to really experience what it would be like.' Then she'd surprised him by taking his hand in hers and giving it a quick squeeze. 'Thank you, Benedict. Today has really felt like a celebration.'

'I'm glad.' He'd lifted her hand to his lips and kissed it. Now as he looked at her sleeping there, her breathing calm and even, Benedict could feel himself slipping further and further towards loving her. It overwhelmed him. When he'd returned from Tarparnii, starting a relationship with any woman had been the last thing on his mind and yet somehow Darla had managed to infiltrate his life and show him just how bright life could be. His past was his past, just as Darla's was hers. Sure, it could sculpt their future but only in a positive way and he felt that with today's activities, with the way she'd handled meeting the rest of his family, it was certainly a step in the right direction. Things were finally changing. He could finally move forward in his life.

'Darla.' He whispered her name and gently rubbed her shoulder but received no response. 'Darla.' He tried again, a little louder, and this time managed to rouse her but only for half a second. She really was dead to the world. He thought for a moment, then reached down to the floor near her feet where she'd put her handbag. 'Sorry,' he murmured as he opened it and peered inside, easily locating her keys. Leaving her in the car, he quickly went and unlocked her door, taking the liberty to go into her room and turn down her bed before returning to the passenger side of the car and carefully opening the door.

He unclipped her seat belt but still she slept on. 'Come on, gorgeous,' he whispered as he managed to scoop her from the seat, carrying her into the house and placing her gently on the bed. Next, he removed her shoes and covered her with the blankets, ensuring the heater was on low to keep her warm through the clear, crisp night. She'd had an emotionally draining day and it had definitely caught up with her.

Benedict stood and watched her for a moment, her blonde hair splayed out on the pillow. She was stunning, both inside and out. She'd been through so much and yet here she was director of a busy A and E department, working hard to fulfil her dreams. He hoped he was part of her dreams because she was definitely part of his. Not only his dreams but his hopes and goals for the future. Tenderly, he brushed a few strands of hair back from her face, then bent and pressed a kiss to her cheek. 'Sleep sweet, my Darla,' he murmured, before heading out, ensuring her house was securely locked before he left.

Darla slowly stretched and breathed out, feeling more content and relaxed than she had in a very long time. There was a smile on her lips and a lightness to her heart and she knew why—Benedict. She reflected on the glorious dreams she'd just had, ones where the two of them walked hand in hand over a grassy oval, sounds of the apple-pie fair all around them, a child between them, holding their hands and jumping around with excitement. Her mind continued to filter through the dream, realising it wasn't one Benedict's nieces or nephews that was between them but *their own child*—a daughter with blonde hair like her mother and blue eyes like her father.

Darla sat bolt upright at the thought, eyes snapping open. She'd been dreaming about living the fairy-tale life with Benedict. He'd been her husband, the little girl had been their daughter and they'd been taking her for the first time to the apple-pie festival, meeting the rest of Benedict's family for a day of fun.

She covered her face with her hands. 'No. No. No. You are *not* to think of a future like that. There *is* no future like that for you. It's just a silly, childish dream. One you've yearned for all your life but you know it'll never happen. You're not meant for a normal life, Darla Fairlie. You're meant to quietly reach out and save others. Quietly helping those who need your help. Marriage and children are *not* your future. Benedict is just a man and men *always* let you down. Be strong. Steer clear. Focus.'

Her words were stern, her mind dictating to her heart the way it was going to be. Her mind had protected her throughout the years whilst her heart had been the one to leap forward and take what she'd thought were chances at happiness…yet all of them had failed.

But Benedict is different, her heart whispered.

No. Her head was adamant and with a satisfied nod she dropped her hands and glanced at the clock. *'Eight-thirty!'* With horror, Darla flicked back the bedcovers and only then realised she was fully dressed. Startled, she stood in the middle of her room, desperately trying to remember what had happened last night. She remembered being in the car, driving away from the best day she'd ever had in her life, Benedict beside her, the radio playing quietly in the background and then…nothing. She couldn't remember arriving home or going to bed.

Shaking her head, she hurried to the bathroom where she showered and dressed. By nine o'clock she was stalking through the entrance doors to the hospital, heading straight to the A and E nurses' station to check on things. Her step faltered when she saw Benedict sitting at the desk, alone, writing up case-notes.

'Hello, gorgeous,' he greeted her when he looked up and saw her standing there.

'Shh,' she hissed, and glanced around lest anyone had heard him.

'It's all right. The department's very quiet at the moment. A calm and comfortable typical-Sunday-morning quiet, rather than an eerie quiet-before-the-storm type of quiet,' he clarified, and stood, intending to lean forward to press a quick kiss to her cheek. Darla placed a hand on his chest, stopping him before he could follow through.

'Not here,' she said between gritted teeth. 'My office. Now.'

Benedict raised his eyebrows with delight. 'Well, if you insist, boss. I'll just finish this and be right with you,' he said, indicating the notes. Darla nodded once and headed to her office, fuming on the inside and wondering why she still couldn't get through to Benedict that she was angry.

She left her office door open but as soon as he appeared, she walked around him, keeping her distance and shutting the door before she turned to glare at him, hands on her hips, foot tapping impatiently.

'What happened?'

Benedict had been about to take her hand in his, hoping she'd let him draw her close for a cuddle. He hadn't been able to stop thinking about her, dreaming about her, wanting her to be with him always, and after yesterday he'd sort of hoped that she might feel the same way. Still, he'd promised not to rush her and it was clear she had a bee in her bonnet. 'What happened when?'

'Last night. This morning.'

'I don't know, Darla. I drove you home, carried you to your bed and left you to sleep.'

'You turned my alarm off.'

'I didn't touch your clock.' He was starting to become concerned. 'What's this all about?'

'It's about me sleeping until eight-thirty this morning!'

'You did? That's great.' He took a step towards her but she held up her hand again.

'Great? No, it's not.'

'It's not?'

'Of course it's not. You should have woken me when we arrived home.'

'Sweetheart, I tried, but you were exhaust—'

'I didn't get up and go to the streets!' she blurted, not caring if she raised her voice. He'd already said there was hardly anyone in the department and right now she didn't even care about that. She had important work to do and she'd failed to do it. She was a horrible person.

'If you'd woken me, I would have been able to set my alarm, to shower before I went to bed, to be ready for when my alarm went off. I could have gone to the streets, I could have talked to more women, I could have saved them.'

'Darla. It's one night and you were exhausted.'

'I don't care about that.'

'I do.' He stepped forward and placed both hands on her shoulders but the instant he made contact she shrugged away from him. 'Darla, you can't expect to go out each and every morning.'

'Yes, I can. I've done it for years now.'

'And how many of those mornings have you come up empty-handed? Unable to get through to people?' he asked.

'That's not the point.'

'Yes, it is. You can't be expected to get through to people every night, and I'm not saying you don't have to keep on persevering and trying because you do, but neither are *you* supposed to be single-handedly saving the world, Darla. There are other people out there who are also helping, like the volunteers with ACT NOW, who are as concerned as you about the state of affairs. Granted, half of us don't have your first-hand knowledge of the situation but a lot of them do. You do amazing work, no one's denying that. You've helped so many women both here and, no doubt, in other States where you've lived. You really are an angel to them, Darla, but you're also human and as such *you* have needs, and one of them is to look after yourself.'

'I don't care about me.'

'Well, I do. I care that you've been working yourself too hard ever since we first met. I'm also guessing yesterday was the first time you've taken time out since arriving in Canberra.'

'You forced me to do it.'

'Because I could see you needed it.'

'I don't need you to tell me what to do, Dr Goldmark. Everything in my world was fine until *you* came along and wrecked it.' She pointed her finger at him. 'I was working at the hospital, I was helping people on the streets in the mornings. I was coping fine and now you… you come along and take me away for apple pie, to meet your family, to show me a world that's real and not just a fairy-tale. You show me how wonderful families can be but it's all a farce. Real life is tough. It's hard. It's hurtful and destructive.' She stabbed herself in the chest with her finger. 'I know this for a fact. There is no happily ever after. There is no "happy families". Not for me. Not ever.' Darla turned her back to him, knowing it didn't matter what she said, she'd never be able to make him understand.

Benedict remained silent for a while before saying softly, 'I said I wouldn't rush you, Darla, and I won't.' Then, to her surprise, she heard the quiet click of the door opening and a moment later another click as it closed behind him. She stood there for a whole two minutes, her back to the door, refusing to allow the tears to fall. It was better this way.

Benedict had been a distraction. A lovely, warm and encompassing distraction but she had a job to do and that job didn't leave any room for distractions. Pain continued to pierce her heart and she pursed her lips together, desperate to fight the overwhelming sense of sorrow flooding through her. She'd pushed him away. It had been the right thing to do. Distance. Focus. Self-control. That was the way to go.

So why did it feel as though she was dying inside?

Darla made herself a cup of tea and was just sipping it when her phone rang. Frowning, she picked it up, hoping it wasn't an emergency at the hospital. It was almost two o'clock in the morning and she was about to head out to the streets. As she'd missed her rounds yesterday, she was eager to get started. 'Dr Fairlie,' she answered.

'Ah, good. You're up.'

'Benedict?'

'Yes. I didn't want to ring your doorbell or knock in case I startled you. I thought calling was the best option and it turns out I was right.'

'What are you talking about? Is there an emergency

at the hospital? Has something gone wrong? Are you all right?' The last one came out before she could stop it.

'Concerned for my well-being, fairy princess? I'm pleased to hear it. No, there's nothing wrong.'

Darla tried not to be affected by the deepness of his voice, the way it sounded like warm chocolate. She sighed and tried to control her thoughts, remembering she'd been mad at him, that she'd pushed him away, shoved him right out of her life. 'Then why are you calling me at this hour?'

'I'm at your front door,' he stated simply.

Darla frowned at her phone, pulling it away from her ear and glaring at it. Was she still sleeping? Dreaming? Why on earth would Benedict be outside her house at two o'clock in the morning?

She returned the phone to her ear, positive he was delusional. 'Benedict. You're making no sense.'

'Look. I'll prove it.' The next instant, Darla could hear knocking at her front door and even though he'd told her he was there, the sound still startled her.

'Benedict!'

'Yes?'

'Is that really you? This isn't just some weird, spooky coinciden—'

'Oh, my giddy aunt. Will you open the door, Darla?'

She walked to the door, cellphone still to her ear. She kept the chain on the door as she opened it slightly, her eyes widening as she saw him standing there. Quickly, she closed the door, removed the chain and opened the door completely.

'Blimey. It's like Fort Knox—but that's good.' He nodded as he disconnected the call and slipped his phone into his jacket pocket. 'Hello.' He stepped forward and

pressed a kiss to her cheek before she even knew which
way was up.

She was dressed in old denim jeans and a comfortable jumper with decent walking shoes on her feet. Her
beautiful blonde hair was pulled back into a ponytail
with a single band. He knew she was trying to down-
play her appearance, to blend into the background, and
he wasn't quite sure whether to tell her she hadn't succeeded. She was far too stunning, no matter what she
wore, to be overlooked, and it was *that* concern for her
safety that had prompted him to be standing in front of
her right now.

Darla blinked once then twice and gave her head a
little shake. 'What are you doing here?' she blurted.

'I'm here to help.'

'But I'm mad at you. I pushed you away. I—'

'Vented your frustrations,' he interrupted. 'I know, I
was there.' He tapped his wrist. 'It's almost two o'clock.
Ready?'

'No. Stop. I don't understand. *Why* are you here?'

'I'm here to help.'

'Help?'

'You know…heading out to the streets? Doing your
angel thing. I thought I could give you a lift. Or we can
go in your car. I'm not fussed.'

'But I was angry at you. I yelled at you,' she reiter-
ated. 'You're not supposed to want to be around me any
more.'

Benedict slowly shook his head, a small smile on his
lips. His actions only caused her eyes to widen and a
fire to light in her belly.

'Don't you dare laugh at me, Benedict Goldmark.'

'I'm not laughing, fairy princess. Don't you have any
idea how gorgeous you are when you're angry?'

She threw her hands in the air and turned to go and collect her jacket. 'You're impossible,' she muttered. When she returned, she found him leaning against the doorjamb, thumbs in the pockets of his jeans, looking casual and relaxed and as sexy as anything. She swallowed over the instant flood of desire that seemed to course through her every time she saw him.

'Go away,' she tried, but he simply shook his head.

'You can be angry at me all you like. You can vent and rant and rave but it doesn't change the way I feel about you.'

'It doesn't?'

She seemed genuinely shocked at that and it gave Benedict a big insight into just how much she really hadn't been able to trust anyone in the past. 'Couples fight. Couples argue. Couples sort things out and then make up.'

'There's nothing to sort out,' she said, frowning as she picked up her keys. 'You and me? We're not a couple. There is no future for us. OK? I am not your girlfriend. You are not my bo—' She stopped and swallowed over the word.

'Boyfriend,' he finished calmly. 'And I want to be more than just your boyfriend. Something far more permanent.'

'A thorn in my side?' she quipped as she pushed past him and headed towards her car, knowing he would close the door behind him. She couldn't deny he looked good, wonderful in fact, and to hear him saying he still wanted to be around her was more than she'd ever expected. Right from day one she'd been unable to control him, unable to freeze him out, unable to resist his hypnotic eyes, his smooth tone and his gorgeous lips.

He was quick and slid into the passenger seat beside

her as she started the engine. 'I hope you have success tonight,' he said softly.

'Stop that.' She glared at him for a moment before putting the car into Reverse.

'Stop what? Hoping that tonight you're able to get through to a woman who needs you? A woman who has lost all hope?'

'I thought you didn't want me going out onto the streets.'

'I've never said that. I've said you shouldn't feel obliged to do it *every* night or else you run the risk of damaging your health. I'll also admit to being a little concerned with you being out in such neighbourhoods alone but—' he quickly continued when she took a breath to interrupt '—I appreciate that you can no doubt spot trouble before it happens. Still, I'm concerned.'

Darla closed her mouth and refused to speak to him until she'd parked the car. 'Don't follow me,' she said as she climbed out, pulling her jacket around her. 'I can look after myself. I know how to fly under the radar. I know about hunger and cold and a burning emptiness deep inside. I know that taking drugs is the coward's way of solving problems and I know that if you come with me right now, you're going to thwart any chances I might have in making a connection and getting someone off the wrong path and onto the right one.' Darla was bristling as she finished talking. Hands on her hips, back straight, chin held high.

Benedict stood in front of her and nodded, placing his hands on her shoulders. 'Just...be safe. OK?' He rested his forehead against hers, his heart churning with an intense surge of love, and he couldn't stop himself from telling her. 'I love you, Darla.'

Darla closed her eyes for a moment, her heart celebrating and breaking all at the same time. She breathed him in then, as she exhaled, she pulled back, stepping away from his embrace. 'Don't. Don't love me, Benedict.' She shook her head sadly. 'I'm no good for you.' With that, she turned and sprinted up the street, away from him.

Benedict couldn't believe how busy they were at the ACT NOW van. Both Jordanne and Hamilton were rostered on with him and the catering van had actually called in extra staff.

'It's a Wednesday night,' Hamilton stated in disbelief as he pulled off one pair of gloves and pulled on another. 'This is ridiculous.' Throughout their shift the van had been so congested that at times they'd had to go outside just to change their minds.

'No.' Benedict shook his head, caution in his tone. 'I've seen this before. This hive of activity. These small spats where people are hurt and require medical attention. There's unrest. Something big has happened somewhere and it's causing a lot of disturbance. We all need to be on guard.'

'When was the last time you saw this?' Jordanne asked as she restocked one of the cupboards.

'On one of the worst nights of my life.' Benedict's words were soft.

'The night Carolina was hurt?' Jordanne guessed.

'Yes.' Benedict checked the clock. He knew Darla was out there. He could just sense it. Ever since the other morning when she'd walked away from him, telling him not to love her, he'd been trying to leave her alone, to give her some space. He was almost positive she felt the same way about him as he did about her. She had to. If she didn't, he thought this time he might really die of a broken heart. She was a good, hardworking, honest woman and he knew she was scared of moving out of the past and into the hope for a new future.

As the angel, she gave advice and hope to those who were in a terrible place, locked in a world of no escape, but she couldn't see that she, too, was still locked into the past, allowing who she'd been while she was growing up to dictate who she needed to be in the future. She wanted the fairy-tale family, as she called it. He'd seen it in her eyes the day they'd gone to the apple-pie fair but she was too scared to take a chance, to risk everything in case she plummeted back into the depths of despair. He had to give her time but he honestly didn't know how much longer he could wait for her to come to her senses. He loved her. She loved him. Surely it *was* that simple?

Concerned, Benedict walked to the door and peered out the van, hoping to see Darla walking towards him, safe and sound, but all he saw were another group of young men heading in their direction, two or three guys, carrying their buddy, who was obviously injured.

'Next round,' Benedict said, after scanning the area once more. Where was she? Which one of these streets was she in? Who was she talking to tonight? Was she safe?

Benedict focused and with Jordanne's orthopaedic expertise they managed to patch the injured man up as well as they could. 'I'm sure you've dislocated your shoulder,' Jordanne stated as she looked at the tattoo of a large, ferocious-looking grizzly bear on the man's arm. 'And you'll need to go to hospital for X-rays to confirm the diagnosis before we can relocate it.'

'Nah. It always pops out,' the guy growled between gritted teeth. 'Put it back.'

'If the head of the bone is fractured, then putting it back in won't do any goo—'

The man bared his teeth, cutting short what Jordanne was going to say. The man in question was about six feet five inches but built like a tank. His arms, neck and upper chest were heavily tattooed and his head was shaved. 'Put it back.'

'I've got this, Jordanne,' Benedict said, and with Hamilton holding the man steady Benedict carefully manipulated the bone back into its socket. The patient didn't yell but instead clenched his teeth and was breathing hard.

Once the bone was back in place, the man started breathing more normally but Benedict could see the pain written on his face. Jordanne checked the shoulder was relocated correctly before prescribing some analgesics.

'Don't want no pills. I don't do drugs any more. Not even paracetamol. I need to get back out there. Lead my gang.'

'Gang?' Benedict's eyebrows hit his hairline. He didn't like the sound of that and once more he scanned outside the vans for any sign of Darla.

'We need to protect them,' one of the men said.

'They're on *our* turf. We got the right to defend it.'

'And I guess we'll just patch you all up and send you back out to risk getting killed again,' Benedict returned, holding the large man's gaze, never wavering. The man didn't look away either but a moment later he surprised them all by grinning.

'You're all right, mate.'

Another young guy who had come with the group of men stuck his head in the van door, agitation clear in his tone. 'Bear. We gotta go. *Now.* The cops are here.'

Bear, the large tattooed man, stood and looked

Benedict, Jordanne and Hamilton in the eyes. 'We'll try and keep you safe, too,' he said firmly.

Within a matter of minutes the van was cleared and Hamilton was setting up for the next round. 'If they're about to fight...'

'We're going to need a lot of back-up,' Jordanne finished. Benedict was looking out the door again. 'What's wrong?'

'Darla,' Benedict replied absent-mindedly. 'She's out there. Somewhere.'

'Why? What on earth is she doing out on the streets at this hour of the morning?' Hamilton asked, completely perplexed.

'She...does...a...' Benedict stopped and tried again. 'She...uh...' How to say it without giving away Darla's secret?

'Oh, my word.' Jordanne gasped, dawning realising in her eyes. 'Blonde hair. Brown eyes. She's *the angel*.'

Benedict closed his eyes for a moment but didn't deny it. Instead he reached for his jacket. 'I need to go and find her, to make sure she's all right, because if anything happens to her...' He trailed off, unable to finish the sentence as his gut was twisted with pain and his mind was flooded with a blinding fury such as he'd never felt before.

Jordanne took one look at him, then nodded. 'Go. Ham and I will be fine here, especially as I'm calling our other team members as well as the authorities to let them know the situation.'

'Good, and put the A and E retrieval team on standby,' Benedict added as he picked up his phone and put it in his pocket.

'Hey, bro. Do you know where to start looking? It's starting to get wild out there.'

'I have an idea.'

Hamilton nodded. 'Stay safe.'

'Likewise,' he murmured with a brisk nod, before stepping from the van and pulling the collar of his jacket up high. He headed towards the street where she usually parked her car, figuring he'd follow the direction she usually went. It wasn't much but it was something.

His shoes echoed on the quiet road, hands shoved into the pockets of his jeans, gaze constantly scanning the area for any sign of her. Where was she? The panic he'd tried hard to control in the van started to wage war within him and he found himself muttering, 'Where are you?' over and over.

It wasn't right for a woman to go traipsing around the streets at such a time of the morning. He didn't care what sort of upbringing she'd had, he didn't care if she held a black belt in karate, it simply wasn't right. She could get hurt, or worse.

'No.' He stopped that thought as he turned down a darkened street. She couldn't be hurt. In his mind he needed to think of her being strong and vibrant because even the slightest thought that she might be lying in the gutter somewhere, hurt, robbed and all alone, turned his mind to mush.

He needed to see for himself that she was all right. Once he'd ascertained that fact, she'd no doubt yell at him about being too overbearing and tell him yet again not to bother loving her. Well, she didn't have a choice in the matter. He loved her and that was all there was to it.

As he turned down an even smaller, even darker side street, still intent on his goal, it was a few minutes before he noticed the group of dark shadows nearby.

'Hey! You!' one of them called, a deep, growling voice. 'Get outta here! This ain't no time for a stroll.'

Benedict frowned. He'd heard that voice before. Another sound echoed behind him and he turned around to find another group of dark shadows coming down the street towards him. He spun again, belatedly realising that due to his focus on finding Darla he'd walked down the wrong street.

'I said get outta here,' the voice growled again.

'Bear?' Benedict was astonished.

'Benedict?' It was Darla's voice. He heard Darla's voice and he spun in the direction he'd thought it had come from. She was all right. She was OK. Alive. Good. Relief flooded through him and a smile lit his face.

The next moment he felt a blinding pain in the back of his head and then his legs seemed unable to hold him up. With white spots flickering before his eyes, he tried to figure out what was going on. Where was Darla? He tried to call her name but he didn't seem able to talk. Pain continued to pound through his head and more shot up his arm. Then everything went black.

CHAPTER ELEVEN

'BENEDICT? Benedict?'

Darla was beside herself as she applied a cold compress to the back of Benedict's head. 'Can't this thing go faster?' she said to the ambulance driver. 'Benedict? Come on. Wake up. I really need you to wake up.'

She clutched his hand in hers, squeezing it tight, desperate for him to open his eyes, to look at her, to let her see that he was all right. He *had* to be all right. He just *had* to be. When she'd seen him go down, hit from behind, her heart had seemed to stop.

For a split second she hadn't known what to do. In all her life, no matter how bad things had been when she'd been growing up, she'd always had a thought, a plan, a course of action. It was how she'd controlled things for so long. Always planning. Always thinking. Always wanting to do whatever she could to find some control.

Then Benedict had been hit. He'd been assaulted by the gang who'd been trying to get to a group of women sheltering in a house. Bear and his gang had been protecting them but Bear had been too late to protect Benedict.

'Benedict?' she called again, tears blurring her vision as the ambulance finally pulled into the hospital. She'd made them call ahead. She'd made them tell the A and E team exactly who was in this ambulance. Everyone in the department loved Benedict…she most of all.

She *loved* him. She could admit it to herself now. She *loved* this man. This impossible, protective, crazy man. He'd somehow managed to break down her defences, he'd accepted her for who she was, and he'd wanted to spend as much time with her as possible.

'Benedict?' she said again, but he remained unconscious. He was wheeled into TR1, with Darla barking out orders to her team, calling for tests and X-rays, and all the while she found it impossible to let go of his hand, even when he was transferred to the hospital barouche.

'Benedict?' she whispered and leaned close. 'Come on. Wake up. I need you…and I don't need anybody.'

The hustle and bustle in the room around her seemed to slow to a snail's pace, everything fading to a blur as she looked down into his handsome face. 'Come on,' she tried again, and this time, not caring in the least who saw, she bent and brushed her lips across his. '*Please?*'

'Darla?' Her name was a choked, dry whisper, barely audible.

'Benedict?' Relief started to flood through her. 'You're OK. Oh, thank God.' She closed her eyes and bowed her head for a moment, wanting to rest it on his shoulder, to put her arms around him, to feel his comforting warmth, but she knew he needed treatment. 'You had me worried.'

'Really? Worried? About me?' He tried to open his eyes but quickly frowned and squinted at the bright lights in the room. 'What happened?'

She straightened up. 'You don't remember?'

'We're ready to take him to Radiology now, Dr Fairlie,' Matrice said.

'Good. Let's go,' she returned, and still holding his hand walked alongside the barouche. As they went along the corridor, Benedict closed his eyes to block out the brightness from the overhead lights. 'Benedict?' she called again.

'I'm here,' he said, his voice a little stronger. 'And I'm glad to see you're OK. You had me worried.'

'Worried?'

'There was a gang war. I couldn't find you.'

Darla momentarily closed her eyes as she began to realise exactly why Benedict had been in that street in the first place. He'd been looking for *her*. Guilt immediately swamped her. He'd been worried about her. He'd come looking for her and he'd been hurt in the process. What was happening to him now was all her fault.

While she waited for him to have X-rays taken, she buried her head in her hands and closed her eyes. It was all her fault. Benedict had been hurt because of her and she vowed it would never happen again.

'Dr Fairlie?' The radiographer spoke quietly and Darla dropped her hands and turned to face the young woman. 'Did you want to see the image on the screen? From what I can see, everything looks fine.'

Darla peered closely at the screen, which displayed the digital image of Benedict's skull. 'It looks clean. Everything's good. No fractures.' Darla straightened and let out a deep breath. 'He's going to be fine.' Tears started to prick behind her eyes and she sniffed, unable to control her rising emotions at this good news.

'Are you all right, Dr Fairlie?' The radiographer was both shocked and startled by this open display of emotion from the ice fairy.

'Uh.' Darla cleared her throat. 'I'm going to my office. Can someone call me when he's back in A and E, please?' She sniffed again, annoyed with herself for losing control and especially in front of a staff member.

'Of course.' There was empathy in the woman's voice accompanied by a small smile. 'I'll make sure of it.'

The woman's kindness threatened to overwhelm Darla and she quickly turned and walked with as much dignity as she could muster towards her office. She pulled her hospital pass-card from her pocket and swiped it through the lock. In another moment she was standing in her office, the door closed behind her, the silent darkness surrounding her.

Benedict was going to be all right. No fracture. No permanent damage, and he also appeared to have excellent recall of events. He was going to be all right. The first sob almost shocked her but as it was closely followed by another, she gave in and allowed herself to cry.

Leaning against the wall, she slowly slumped down to the floor, the picture of him standing there in the street running through her mind. The shock, the fear, the terror at seeing a dark shadow come up behind him before it attacked. She closed her eyes tighter, desperate to block out the image as her body was racked with another spasm of pain.

'Oh, Benedict,' she murmured. She hugged her knees to her chest, unable to believe how much she was hurting. She'd known she had serious feelings for the man but now she could clearly recognise and admit to herself that she was in love with him. There were no two ways about it. She loved Benedict Goldmark.

Somehow the man had managed to get beneath her skin, to infiltrate her carefully constructed walls and make her care about him. She'd fought it. She'd tried to keep her distance but he hadn't let her. He'd been all cute and charming and gorgeous and…and…

'And I have to let you go,' she whispered into the dark. 'No fairy-tales for Darla Fairlie.' Loving him wasn't part of her plan. Becoming involved with Benedict's life would only cause them both more pain in the long run and she loved him too much to let that happen.

'I'm fine,' Benedict implored as his brothers fussed over him like two old women. 'Seriously. A few stitches and I'm fine. See?' He showed them both the back of his head where a sterile white bandage covered the ten sutures in his head. 'It's not the first time I've had sutures.'

'True,' Bart relented, and Hamilton sat down, lounging in the chair beside the bed. 'It's a hard habit to break—caring for my brothers.'

'I'm not asking you to break it, bro, just tone it down. You're as bad as Mum used to be.'

Bart grinned. 'I'll take that as a compliment.'

'Now, tell me, Ham, what happened after I was knocked out? Is everything settled now? Did the police manage to get everything under control? Jordanne? Is she all right?'

He looked through the glassed walls of his private room into the ward, as though expecting their friend to immediately materialise. Secretly, he also knew he was searching for Darla. Where was she? When he'd returned from Radiology back to A and E she'd come into the treatment room to check on him but this time, instead of being the woman who had held his hand and kissed him ever so tenderly, she was the ice fairy once more. He scanned the nurses' station but there was no sign of her. Where was she?

'Everything's sorted. Jordanne's fine. By the time the police were in position it was basically all over. That guy who dislocated his shoulder—Bear—was the leader of

the gang protecting a group of women who were sheltering in one of the houses in the street. Bear brought in
three from his gang for us to fix and told us how sorry
he was you'd been hurt.' Hamilton nodded. 'He's a good
guy. Rough as guts but a good guy nonetheless.'

Ward Sister walked into the private room and stood
there, crossing her arms over her chest and tapping her
foot. 'What are the two of you still doing here?'

'Talking to our brother?' Hamilton offered.

'Bringing him some clothes,' Bart said at the same
time.

'He's had enough excitement for the moment and
has to rest. Come along. Bartholomew, I'm sure you
have a ward round to attend and, Hamilton, you look
as though you could use a shower and some sleep. Off
you go. Leave your brother in peace so he can rest.'

'I don't know why I have to stay,' Benedict grumbled.
'I'm perfectly all right.'

'I don't care what you say, Ben, it's doctor's orders
and they state quite clearly that you're to be kept in
for observation for the next twenty-four hours at least,'
Ward Sister returned in her usual brisk manner. Benedict
frowned. Usually he was able to charm the woman, to
get a smile from her, to get her to bend the rules a little
here and there, but not now. She was adamant that he
was not only to stay in bed until he was properly discharged by his admitting doctor but also that his brothers needed to leave in order to allow him to get some
rest.

'You're not a colleague now, Benedict,' Sister continued, as though she could read his mind. 'You're my patient. This is my ward and you will obey me.' She turned
to glare at Bart and Hamilton. 'And you two—go.'

'OK. OK.' Hamilton held up his hands in defence. 'We'll let the poor old soul rest.'

'Thank you. Now I need to see to the breakfasts.' She bustled the brothers out and then closed the blinds to the room. 'Get some rest, Ben.'

'Yes, Sister,' he replied meekly as he closed his eyes. He was sure he wasn't tired, sure he would be wide awake and completely bored before the breakfast trolley had made its rounds, but with the room now nice and dark and relatively quiet Benedict found his eyes becoming heavier.

The next time he opened his eyes, for a moment, he wasn't sure where he was. Lying still, he slowly took in his surroundings. He was in the hospital. As a patient. The events leading up to him being there flooded through his mind and as he shifted slightly, he tried not to wince in pain.

'Try and stay still.' A sweet, angelic voice spoke from somewhere on his right and he had to force himself to slowly turn his head. There she was. The angel. *His* angel.

'Darla?'

'I'm here.'

'What time is it?'

'Just after two in the afternoon. You've been sleeping quite nicely.'

'Where were you?' he asked.

'In my office, catching up on some paperwork. That little melee brought us quite a few casualties but, thankfully, there were no fatalities.'

'No, I mean before. On the streets. I couldn't find you and I was so worried and concerned and—'

'Shh.' She leaned forward and placed a finger gently on his lips. 'You're fine. I'm fine. That's all that mat-

ters now.' It wasn't until she went to remove her hand
that she realised just how close she was to the man she
loved. What was it about him that simply drew her in?
How was she supposed to resist him, especially now
when he was lying in a hospital bed with sutures in his
skull?

'Darla.'

Benedict somehow looked directly into her soul, his
magnetic allure drawing her closer as he continued to
hypnotise her with his soothing voice and come-hither
eyes. The urge to follow was overpowering and when
he reached out to tuck a loose tendril of hair back behind her ear, she was completely captivated.

She loved him. He loved her. He'd said he wouldn't
pressure her. He'd said he'd allow her to take her time
and she knew that he would continue to keep his distance if she asked. Right now, she didn't want him to
and realised it would be nothing to close the distance
between them. Following through on her selfish urge,
Darla leaned closer and within the next moment had
pressed her mouth firmly to his.

She closed her eyes and sighed at the touch, not realising how much she'd missed feeling these sensations,
the ones she only felt when Benedict was kissing her.
This time, though, there was something different about
the way he kissed her, about the way he cradled the back
of her head with his hand, his fingers instantly working her hair from her sensible ponytail. His mouth was
more familiar, his touch more intense, and his previously reined-in hunger was bursting forth.

He wanted to show her, to let her feel just how important she was to him. Her lips were parting, accepting
his advances as he continued to devour the deliciousness
of this incredible woman. Step by step, moment by mo-

ment. She kept pace with him, appearing to want him just as much as he wanted her. It was what he'd been waiting for, the realisation that they were made for each other.

When he groaned, she instantly pulled back, breathing hard as she frantically scanned his face. 'What's wrong? Did I hurt you? I'm sorry, Benedict. I didn't mean to get you hurt. Do you want some analgesics?' Her words ran over each other, fear and trepidation flooding through her.

'I'm fine,' he muttered quickly, before urging her lips back to where they belonged—against his own. 'Darla. Darla. You are so beautiful, so caring and warm,' he murmured against her mouth between kisses. 'I can't stop loving you.'

'You must,' she implored.

'No. I can't and I won't.'

Darla straightened up and moved away from the bed. Benedict reached for her hand but she was able to avoid his touch.

'Darla, I'm sorry if that scares you but it's the truth. I can't hide it from you any more.'

'Yes, you can.' She was astonished to find her legs trembling as though they were made of jelly. 'Hide it. Quash it. Forget it.' She shook her head. 'Don't love me, Benedict. It doesn't work.'

'What doesn't work?' he asked, raising his voice slightly in complete exasperation. A moment later he scowled at the sudden pounding in his head.

'Will you stay calm?' she scolded, worry in her tone. 'You'll give yourself an even bigger headache.'

'I don't care.'

Darla picked up the small container of tablets that

had been left by his bed and handed them to him, before pouring a glass of water. 'Take these.'

'I'm fine.'

'I'm your doctor and you'll take them.' Darla stood over him and he knew she wouldn't let him move on, explain himself, make her understand just how important she was to him until he did as he was told.

'You know, you could discharge me. I can convalesce at home quite easily.'

'But you wouldn't stay still,' Darla countered, replacing the glass back on the bedside table once he'd done as he was told.

'So you're keeping me in for extended observation because you don't think I'll follow your orders?'

'I *know* you wouldn't.' Darla stepped back from the bed and crossed her arms. She stared at him and Benedict stared right back, trying to read her, trying to figure out why she didn't want him to love her.

'You want me where you can monitor me,' he stated.

'Yes.'

'Because you care about me.'

Darla's gaze flickered for a moment but she eventually nodded her head.

'But you don't care about me enough to accept the love I have for you?' His words were quieter this time and she sucked in a breath, squaring her shoulders and standing firm beneath his gentle scrutiny.

'Why, Darla?' he asked softly. 'Why aren't I allowed to love you?'

'Because it will only bring heartache and pain to us both.' She turned and took a step towards the door. 'Go back to sleep.'

'If you leave now, I'll get out of this bed and follow you,' he threatened. Darla looked at him over her shoulder and saw he was lifting the bedcovers. She didn't want him walking about the hospital, not just yet. She wanted him to recover, to be safe, to be secure, and she could only ensure that by keeping him under her watchful eye until she was positive he was really OK. He was slowly moving his legs beneath the covers, getting ready to swing them out.

'All right,' she said, and turned back to face him, her arms still crossed in an effort to protect herself from his delicious gaze.

'Thank you.' He indicated the chair. 'Won't you sit down?'

'I'm fine standing.'

'OK. So, why am I not allowed to love you, Darla?'

She smiled at his words and rolled her eyes. 'Straight to the point.'

'I don't see any reason to beat about the bush. I've confessed my love, you've rejected it. I think I'm entitled to know why, considering I'm fairly sure you love me back.'

'Arrogance,' she muttered.

'Yep.' He didn't waver, didn't lower his eyes, just kept looking at her, firm and sure in his words.

'Why? How could you possibly be in love with me?' Her voice was soft and he could hear the apprehension in her tone.

Benedict's eyes widened as the words rushed out of her mouth, all her insecurities on display for him to see. 'Darla.' He held out his hand. 'Come here.'

'No.'

Benedict dropped his hand. 'OK. Then why don't you sit down and tell me why you think you shouldn't be loved?'

'Because I'm not worthy of it.' She spread her arms

wide, exasperation powering through her. 'Because I'm not a nice person. If you knew half the things I've done in my past...' She rubbed a hand across her forehead, fear in her eyes.

'That's the past. It doesn't matter.'

'No, Benedict. My past is a part of me and I know when you find out, you'll stop loving me. Your love for me is a lie but you can't see it. It's why I can't be around you, why you need to forget me.'

Benedict held out his hand again and shifted over to make room for her to sit beside him. 'Please come here. Please?'

Closing her eyes for a moment, she knew the time had finally come to let go of this man. She would tell him the truth, she would be open and honest, answering all his questions, and then he would see she was no good...and leave. Even the thought of him not being in her life brought a stabbing pain to her heart.

Opening her eyes, she dragged in a breath and then nodded then slowly walked towards him. She accepted his hand and sat on the side of his bed.

'Thank you. Now, what is it you've been hiding for far too long?'

'Me. I've been hiding me.'

'Hiding behind your past?'

'Yes. You've called me on it before, Benedict, and I've managed to keep you at bay, but when you say you love me, I don't have any defences left. I've been fighting my past for so long that if I let go of it...what am I supposed to cling to?'

'Us. You cling to us.' Benedict brushed a hand across her cheek. 'Let go of the past, Darla. Come with me into the present so we can build a wonderful future together.

I can promise to be there for you, I can offer you my heart and my love, but it's up to you to accept it.'

'That's the point, Benedict. I don't know if I can.'

'But do you want to?'

'Yes.' The word was filled with vehement conviction.

'Then do it. Take that chance, Darla. Take the chance with me. Hand in hand we'll walk together.' He pulled her close, wrapping his arms around her. Darla shifted to untangle her legs and belatedly realised she was lying down beside him, his arms firm about her shaky body.

'I want to hold you in my arms and protect you. I want to make sure that no one else *ever* hurts you again. I want to show you how easy you are to love, how important you are not only as a person but as a desirable woman.' He dropped a kiss to the top of her head and held her, wanting his actions to mirror his words. 'Darla, I love you. Can you at least accept that?'

'Yes.'

'Can you accept that even if you want me to stop, I can't. You are *it*.' He shrugged his shoulders. 'There is no other woman I will ever love as much as I love you. There is no other woman who can make me as happy as you do. I watched my parents have a happy and healthy marriage and even in death they were still together. Morbid as it sounds, that's always brought me comfort. My brothers Peter and Edward, as well as Lorelai, have all found long and lasting loves and that's what I want for us. I choose to be with you for the rest of my life and I desperately hope you want the same.'

Tenderly, he stroked her hair, brushing it from her face so he could look down into the deep brown eyes of the woman he adored. 'I love you, Darla. Nothing is ever going to change that. Do you believe me?'

'I want to,' she whispered. 'I really want to, Benedict.'

'Do you love me?'

Darla opened her mouth to say the words, knowing he could see it clearly reflected in her eyes, but there were also many years of locking her heart and emotions away that still needed to be overcome.

Benedict chuckled when she didn't respond and again Darla was perplexed. He never seemed to respond in the way she expected. 'All right, then, how about this? Blink one long blink if you love me.'

Darla immediately blinked her eyes, opening them to gaze into his.

'That's what I thought,' he murmured as he lowered his mouth to brush a tantalising and seductive kiss across her lips. 'Now, how about one long blink if you really want to spend the rest of your life with me?'

Darla bit her lip, hesitating only because with everything she'd endured during her life this was the scariest thing she'd ever done. She closed her eyes, sighed deeply, then opened them to look into the kind, caring and caressing eyes of the man of her dreams. She was rewarded with another, sweet and glorious kiss, this one a little longer than before.

'I want to marry you, my darling Darla. We'll take things slowly and steadily, savouring every new step together. Does that sound good?'

Darla nodded and gave one long blink at the same time. Benedict brought his mouth to hers, lingering, taking his time and letting her know he was serious about taking it slowly. Slowly and sensually. Darla deserved to be cherished and he was just the man to do it.

Without warning, she jerked back and glared at him, her eyes wide with terror. 'What about children?' she gasped. 'What if you want them and I don't? What if I accidentally get pregnant? What if I can't have children at all? Benedict?'

'Slow…and…steady,' he said softly, punctuating his words with kisses. 'I come from a big family, Darla, with my siblings presently populating like rabbits.' He chuckled as he said the words. 'If we decide not to have a family, there will always be plenty of nieces and nephews to spoil.'

'Really?'

'I will never lie to you, Darla. With you in my life, I am a happy and contented man. I also understand how important your work is. The way you help those women is a gift and one that should be nurtured. I'll do whatever I can to assist *the angel*.' He winked at her.

'Oh, Benedict.' Darla sighed and relaxed back into his arms. 'I knew you were trouble from the first moment we met.'

'Trouble?'

She kissed his mouth and laughed, feeling light-hearted and free for the first time in her life. Benedict hadn't been permanently hurt. He loved her. He wanted to marry her, to be with her, to help her. He accepted her for who she was and what she could give. Never in her life had she ever thought she could be *this* happy. Benedict had integrated himself into her life, into her heart, and she'd never been more pleased with the trouble he'd caused her. 'Trouble,' she confirmed.

'Is that a good thing?' he asked, still a little uncertain.

Darla laughed, feeling the shackles of her past float away as she moved towards her future. Benedict. The man of her dreams. 'Is that a good thing?' She echoed his words as she leaned forward to kiss him once more. 'Most definitely.'

EPILOGUE

A FEW weeks later they headed back to Oodnaminaby for little Susan's christening.

'I'm nervous,' Darla confessed when they were about five minutes away from the Ood turn-off.

'Nervous? Why?' he asked, glancing across at her. 'You've met my siblings before and they all love you.'

'Yes but we're...you know...more than we were before.'

'I think the word you're looking for is *engaged*.'

'Yes, we're engaged.' She forced herself to say the word. Every morning it was a constant challenge for her to accept this new life she'd been granted. She had a man who adored her and wanted to spend the rest of his life with her. Through him she was being given the big fairy-tale family she'd always dreamed about. She was incredibly happy yet at the same time she was having difficulty in accepting all these blessings.

After Benedict had been discharged from the hospital, before he'd even returned home, he'd insisted they head to a jewellery store to buy her ring. Darla had been scared and thrilled and excited and nervous all at the same time.

'This is you not rushing things?' she'd asked as they'd stood outside the store.

'I just don't want you to change your mind,' he'd confessed, showing her his insecurity. 'I want you to choose
the ring, to have something *you* love, rather than what I
might choose. If you don't want to wear it straight away,
you don't have to. If you don't want to tell people straight
away, you don't have to. Just so long as you and I know,
that's all that matters.'

So they'd looked at rings and, quite to her own surprise, Darla found the most perfect engagement ring. It
was white gold with a single, solitary diamond in a bezel
setting. In fact, it had been Benedict who had pointed
it out. 'I think this one would look perfect on your fingers. Stunning and elegant. Just like you.' He'd pressed
a kiss to her lips, then winked.

The shop assistant had handed it to Benedict who had
slipped it onto her finger. It had looked perfect, too perfect, and for one split second Darla had started to panic
again. She'd glanced up at Benedict, who had merely
smiled encouragingly, his eyes projecting a mix of security and tranquillity that had miraculously allayed all
her fears.

She'd looked back at the ring, then nodded. 'This is
the one.'

'Would you like to wear it?' the sales assistant had
asked. Again, Darla had looked at Benedict, unsure what
he wanted. Did he want her to wear it? Would he be of-
fended if she took it off and kept it in a box?

'We'll take it in the box,' he'd stated, not breaking
eye contact with her. After they'd left the shop, they'd
driven to his favourite bakery where he'd introduced her
to his friend Tom. Over coffee and her favourite blue-
berry muffin, he'd presented her with the box.

'Darla, I want you to take your time. This is only a
symbol of my love. It can't capture the surging torrent

of eternal love coursing through me but so long as you know I am yours, for ever, that's all I need.'

Furiously blinking back tears, she'd accepted his vow and the box. Right now she had the box in her jacket pocket, her ringless fingers held warmly in his. He indicated to turn off to Ood and all too soon he brought the car to a stop outside his family home. He switched off the ignition and turned to face her. 'Don't be nervous, my darling Darla. This is good. This is right. This is meant to be.'

'I know.'

'Come on,' he urged, and unclipped their seat belts. 'The longer we sit out here, the more we risk them all trooping out to see what's taking us so long.' He leaned over and lovingly kissed her lips, before climbing out and coming around to the open her door. He took her hand in his again and as they walked up the driveway, Darla marvelled at the large two-storey house surrounded by the beautiful colours of late autumn. It was perfect.

They went up the front steps and in through the door, Darla feeling strange at not knocking. The first thing that hit her as they entered was the noise. Children running and laughing, voices, both male and female, all talking over each other. The sweet smells of home cooking coming from the kitchen and the widest smile ever on Benedict's face.

This was Benedict's home and this time she would be here with his entire family. Last time, for the apple-pie fair, Hamilton and Bartholomew had still been in Canberra and Lorelai's father had been at work. Now everyone was here and everyone would be wanting to know the status of her relationship with Benedict. She tried not to feel pressured and the ring box felt like a lead weight in her jacket pocket.

'Ben! Darla! Finally.' Honeysuckle ran towards them both, her arms out wide as she embraced them. 'What took you so long?

No sooner had Honey welcomed her than Darla found herself embraced in another hug, this time by Benedict's surrogate sister, Lorelai. After Lorelai came Peter's wife Annabelle, then Darla was introduced to BJ and was surprised when even he embraced her with a warm hug.

'Welcome to the family,' he'd stated with a wink.

'Benedict?' Darla had looked at her fiancé in surprise. 'You told them?' she whispered.

BJ obviously heard her remark because he laughed. 'Oh, Darla. Your feelings for Ben are written all over your face. It's clear the two of you are in love.' With that, he was distracted by his granddaughter, leaving Darla completely stunned.

'Is it?' she asked Benedict. 'Is it written all over my face?'

He smiled. 'I hope so. This is family, Darla. You're safe here. Just relax and enjoy the ride.'

And what a ride it was! It was a loud, vibrant and energetic household and at times more than a little overwhelming. After a few hours, with Benedict standing at the dishwasher, chatting to his brother Edward as they stacked it with yet another load of plates, Darla slipped out the back door, needing just a brief moment of peace.

She headed out to the little garden, pleased to find it empty. Sitting down on the small bench, she closed her eyes and drew in a few calming breaths. It was what she'd wanted, the fairy-tale family, and she was sure she'd get used to it in time. It was all happening. All her dreams were coming true and as she opened her eyes and looked out over the lovely township of Oodnaminaby, she knew, even though it was completely overwhelming at times, it was the best thing that had ever happened to her. *Benedict* was the best thing that had ever happened to her.

Slowly, she withdrew the box from her pocket and took out the ring. She held it between her forefingers and thumbs, watching the different colours in the diamond as the afternoon sun's rays reflected through it.

'I thought I'd find you here.' Benedict's soft words floated around her as he walked down the small steps that led to the garden.

'This place is beautiful.' Darla didn't move. She was still holding the ring but allowing her gaze to encompass the surrounding garden.

'I love it. We all do. It makes us feel close to Mum. I can still picture her out here. Planting, weeding, drawing secrets from me.'

'She sounds wonderful.'

Benedict nodded. 'She was. She was a doctor. She was a mother. She was a helper. She was a friend. She was amazing and you, my darling Darla, remind me a lot of her.' Benedict came and sat down beside her.

'I do?'

'Yes. Maybe not in looks because she had dark hair, but in personality most definitely.'

'Do you think she would have—?'

'Liked you?' he finished when she broke off. 'Without a doubt.'

They sat in silence for a few minutes before Darla suddenly stood and turned to face him, surprising Benedict further when she went down on one knee. 'What are you doing?' he asked.

'Shh.'

'Right.'

Darla took a moment to gather her thoughts before she held out the ring to him. 'Please hold it with me.' He did as she suggested, the two of them holding the engagement ring between them. She cleared her throat. 'Benedict…' She paused and blinked her eyes in one slow, long blink. 'I…'

He waited.

'I…'

He silently urged her on, wanting her to overcome her fear of completely trusting another person. During the past few weeks she'd been accepting of his touches and kisses and quiet talks as they'd discussed their plans for the future. He'd known she'd say the words when she was ready and it appeared now was the time.

'I…love you.' She breathed a sigh of relief then laughed as silly tears came into her eyes. 'Oh, my goodness, I *love* you. I love you. I love you. *I love you!*' She laughed again. 'I had no idea I would feel *this* free. I love you, Benedict Goldmark. I love you so much and I want desperately to be your wife. Your lover, your friend, your soulmate. I want to bear witness to your life, to all those little intimate moments you'll share with no one else but me. I want to be together for a very long time, to grow old, to continue helping others throughout our lifetime.'

Darla heaved another enormous sigh, then looked from Benedict to the ring. 'Please place this on my finger so everyone will know it's a token of the love we share.'

'With pleasure,' he murmured, and slipped the ring onto the third finger on her left hand. 'I love you, Darla. So very much.'

'And I love you.' With that, he pulled her to her

feet, standing beside her and wrapping his big protective arms about her, drawing her close and pressing his
mouth to hers in a true and honest kiss that would bind
their lives together—for ever.

* * * * *

ROMANCE

A Vow of Obligation	Lynne Graham
Defying Drakon	Carole Mortimer
Playing the Greek's Game	Sharon Kendrick
One Night in Paradise	Maisey Yates
His Majesty's Mistake	Jane Porter
Duty and the Beast	Trish Morey
The Darkest of Secrets	Kate Hewitt
Behind the Castello Doors	Chantelle Shaw
The Morning After The Wedding Before	Anne Oliver
Never Stay Past Midnight	Mira Lyn Kelly
Valtieri's Bride	Caroline Anderson
Taming the Lost Prince	Raye Morgan
The Nanny Who Kissed Her Boss	Barbara McMahon
Falling for Mr Mysterious	Barbara Hannay
One Day to Find a Husband	Shirley Jump
The Last Woman He'd Ever Date	Liz Fielding
Sydney Harbour Hospital: Lexi's Secret	Melanie Milburne
West Wing to Maternity Wing!	Scarlet Wilson

HISTORICAL

Lady Priscilla's Shameful Secret	Christine Merrill
Rake with a Frozen Heart	Marguerite Kaye
Miss Cameron's Fall from Grace	Helen Dickson
Society's Most Scandalous Rake	Isabelle Goddard

MEDICAL

Diamond Ring for the Ice Queen	Lucy Clark
No.1 Dad in Texas	Dianne Drake
The Dangers of Dating Your Boss	Sue MacKay
The Doctor, His Daughter and Me	Leonie Knight

Mills & Boon® Large Print

May 2012

ROMANCE

The Man Who Risked It All	Michelle Reid
The Sheikh's Undoing	Sharon Kendrick
The End of her Innocence	Sara Craven
The Talk of Hollywood	Carole Mortimer
Master of the Outback	Margaret Way
Their Miracle Twins	Nikki Logan
Runaway Bride	Barbara Hannay
We'll Always Have Paris	Jessica Hart

HISTORICAL

The Lady Confesses	Carole Mortimer
The Dangerous Lord Darrington	Sarah Mallory
The Unconventional Maiden	June Francis
Her Battle-Scarred Knight	Meriel Fuller

MEDICAL

The Child Who Rescued Christmas	Jessica Matthews
Firefighter With A Frozen Heart	Dianne Drake
Mistletoe, Midwife...Miracle Baby	Anne Fraser
How to Save a Marriage in a Million	Leonie Knight
Swallowbrook's Winter Bride	Abigail Gordon
Dynamite Doc or Christmas Dad?	Marion Lennox

Mills & Boon® Hardback

June 2012

ROMANCE

A Secret Disgrace	Penny Jordan
The Dark Side of Desire	Julia James
The Forbidden Ferrara	Sarah Morgan
The Truth Behind his Touch	Cathy Williams
Enemies at the Altar	Melanie Milburne
A World She Doesn't Belong To	Natasha Tate
In Defiance of Duty	Caitlin Crews
In the Italian's Sights	Helen Brooks
Dare She Kiss & Tell?	Aimee Carson
Waking Up In The Wrong Bed	Natalie Anderson
Plain Jane in the Spotlight	Lucy Gordon
Battle for the Soldier's Heart	Cara Colter
It Started with a Crush...	Melissa McClone
The Navy Seal's Bride	Soraya Lane
My Greek Island Fling	Nina Harrington
A Girl Less Ordinary	Leah Ashton
Sydney Harbour Hospital: Bella's Wishlist	Emily Forbes
Celebrity in Braxton Falls	Judy Campbell

HISTORICAL

The Duchess Hunt	Elizabeth Beacon
Marriage of Mercy	Carla Kelly
Chained to the Barbarian	Carol Townend
My Fair Concubine	Jeannie Lin

MEDICAL

Doctor's Mile-High Fling	Tina Beckett
Hers For One Night Only?	Carol Marinelli
Unlocking the Surgeon's Heart	Jessica Matthews
Marriage Miracle in Swallowbrook	Abigail Gordon

Mills & Boon® Large Print

June 2012

ROMANCE

HISTORICAL

MEDICAL

0512 GEN STD LP